O Connell

Conferences on the Blessed Trinity

O Connell

Conferences on the Blessed Trinity

ISBN/EAN: 9783741188381

Manufactured in Europe, USA, Canada, Australia, Japa

Cover: Foto ©Andreas Hilbeck / pixelio.de

Manufactured and distributed by brebook publishing software
(www.brebook.com)

O Connell

Conferences on the Blessed Trinity

CONFERENCES

ON THE

BLESSED TRINITY.

BY

THE REV. DR. J. J. O'CONNELL, O.S.B.,

ST. MARY'S COLLEGE, GASTON CO., N. C.

NEW YORK :

THE CATHOLIC PUBLICATION SOCIETY CO.,

9 BARCLAY STREET.

1882.

TO THE

Most Holy and Undivided Trinity,

ONE GOD

IN THREE DIVINE PERSONS,

THE FATHER, AND THE SON, AND THE HOLY GHOST,

WHO ARE REALLY DISTINCT AND EQUAL IN ALL THINGS,

THIS HUMBLE TRIBUTE IS REVERENTLY OFFERED,

THROUGH THE

Immaculate Virgin Mother,

AS AN ACT OF THE MOST FIRM FAITH IN THE

ADORABLE MYSTERY,

BY

THE LAST AND LEAST OF HIS CHILDREN,

JEREMIAH JOSEPH O'CONNELL, O.S.B.

———————

" THESE THREE ARE ONE "—1 JOHN v. 7.

FACULTAS PRÆLATI REGULARIS.

Imprimatur:

BONIFACIUS,

Abbas et Præses Congreg.

Datum a Collegio Sanctæ Mariæ, in comitatu Gastoniensis, Carolinæ Septentri-
onalis, Festo Sancti Joannis ante Portam Latinam, A.D. 1882.

TABLE OF CONTENTS.

	PAGE
DEDICATION, ...	3
APPROBATION, ...	4
AUTHORS, ...	7
PREFATORY EPISTLE TO JAMES McMAHON, ESQ., . . .	9

CONFERENCE I.

| On God's Existence, ... | 15 |

CONFERENCE II.

| On the Divine Perfections, ... | 51 |

CONFERENCE III.

| On the Divinity of our Lord Jesus Christ, . | 88 |

CONFERENCE IV.

| On the Divinity of our Lord Jesus Christ (continued), . . | 119 |

CONFERENCE V.

| On the Divinity and Procession of the Holy Ghost, . . | 150 |

CONFERENCE VI.

| On the Blessed Trinity in Unity of Divine Nature, . . | 180 |

CONFERENCE VII.

| On Creation, ... | 207 |

CONFERENCE VIII.

| On the Real Presence, ... | 235 |

AUTHORS.

The following works were consulted in compiling this volume, and have furnished much material; a general indebtedness is gratefully acknowledged without special quotations:

Archbishop Kenrick's Theology.
Perrone's Theology.
Petavius on the Trinity.
Lessius on the Divine Attributes.
Bibliotheca Patrum.
Summa of St. Thomas.
City of God—St. Augustine.
Suarez de Deo.
Fénelon on the Existence of God.
Bishop England's Works.
Bossuet's Works.
Massillon's Sermons.
Lelandais' Sermons.
Father Gratry's Works.
The Gentle Sceptic—Father Walworth.
Cardinal Wiseman's Lectures.
Father Faber's Works.
The Spiritual Exercises of St. Ignatius—Bellecius.

The Pastoral of Archbishop Joly.
Pastoral of Archbishop Desprez.
Cardinal Billiot's Works.
Cardinal Manning's Sermons.
Cardinal Newman's Sermons.
Archbishop Gibbons's Faith of Our Fathers.
Fletcher's Sermons.
Abbé Noel's Sermons.
Abbé Perraud's Discourses.
Definitions of the Vatican Council.
American Catholic Quarterly Review.
The Catholic World, and many other sources.

PREFATORY EPISTLE

TO

JAMES MCMAHON, ESQ., BROOKLYN, N. Y.

MY DEAR AND ESTEEMED FRIEND:

This treatise embraces lectures and sermons delivered frequently during a period of thirty-eight years in the holy ministry, and varying in length, style, and form to suit the characters of the different audiences. Honored with the chair of theology in this college, the class recitations and doctrinal discussions have given the theses their present title and shape. At the request of several friends I now offer them for perusal to the American people, and in fact to all serious readers, whether Catholic or non-Catholic.

At one time it was hoped that after the turbulent so-called Reformation should have spent itself, and after people should be disabused of the errors brought about by the "Reforma-

1

tion," the greater number would return to the faith of their fathers—to THE ONE TRUE FOLD. Such, unfortunately, has not been the case. It is true the masses of the people of Western Europe did not formally apostatize; their faith was stolen from them; they were in reality cheated of their bright inheritance. And this was an additional ground for hope. Never deciding for themselves, only a national revolution could convert them. But the more recent upheavings of society wear their face in a different direction.

Infidelity and intellectual impiety are daily increasing more and more; and though, with some exceptions, not formally our national and characteristic sins, the common attitude in the United States towards God is worldliness and indifference. An insatiable thirst for wealth, humanitarianism, self-laudation, a growing tendency to free-love, and a merely outward respect for worship of some sort are striking features of non-Catholic society.

This treatise is published with the purpose of contravening these evils, and of serving as an antidote to the fast-increasing intellectual impiety of this otherwise happy land. The weakest barrier against irreligion, even the bare assertion of the truth, can scarcely fail to produce some though partial good; it will at least excite a good thought somewhere, the value of which all the doctors of theology could never fully comprehend nor adequately explain.

Although they have been ably and more fully written by others, I have, at great pains, systematized some of the leading truths of religion, and I have compressed the proofs into a moderate-sized volume that will be accessible to most readers. I have presented the chief arguments in their simplest form and in an unbroken connection, one supporting the other or else flowing from it as a logical consequence and constituting a system that cannot fail to impress the mind of the serious and well-disposed reader in favor of our adorable faith, and perhaps subdue wandering thoughts in the mind of the Christian which tease if they do not assail his belief. This substantial abridgment of the principal proofs of THE MOST SUBLIME MYSTERY, though necessarily concise, is sufficiently comprehensive to be clear, and it enables the reader to take in at a glance the entire structure of the arguments.

There are eight Conferences on the Blessed Trinity: they embrace the Existence of God the Father; the Divine Perfections; the Divinity of our Lord Jesus Christ; the Divinity and Procession of the Holy Ghost; the Trinity of Persons in the Divine Unity. Here, perhaps, the treatise might end; but I have added two other Conferences, one on the Creation and the other on the Blessed Eucharist—that is to say, on the greatest works of God, because of their inaccessible heights, closely allied to the mystery of the Most Holy Trinity and to the works of all the divine Persons combined, like all other operations, with this difference: that the Blessed Eucharist is God Himself and is what the Church styles in the Holy Mass THE MYSTERY OF FAITH by excellence.

To relieve the labor of pondering on arguments found in the region of pure truth I have interwoven moral reflections suggested by the mysteries, and no less for the instruction and edification of the student or pious reader. Without the safeguard of prayer St. Paul assures us that science *puffs up*.

I have studiously avoided all subtilties and school questions, which seldom edify, but administer rather to curiosity, and which have often been formalized into ·heresies. Surely we should be contented with what has been defined by the Church as of faith and with what we certainly know. Every doctrine of the Church claims the homage and adoration of angels and saints for time and eternity.

All these Conferences are suitable for the pulpit, and have been preached by myself with much advantage to the people. Too long in their present shape, I have divided each and have numbered the points at which the enlightened clergyman can break off, to continue the argument on another occasion without detriment to the unity of the subject. This has been my plan.

I have taken great pains to secure accuracy, but if all the notes and quotations were exhibited the book would swell to an inconvenient bulk. I have, therefore, given without special references a summary of most of the authors consulted.

The volume is published with your co-operation and through your zeal for the diffusion of the knowledge which is in Christ Jesus, and I trust, therefore, that you will reap an abundant reward.

I submit the volume without any reserve and in all respects to the judgment of the Holy Catholic Church and her Infallible Head, the Pope ; and I disavow beforehand any propositions that may be at variance with the authorized teachings of our Holy Mother the Church.

I have the honor to be, my dear Mr. Mc-
Mahon, your devoted friend in Christ,

J. J. O'CONNELL, O.S.B.

BENEDICTINE MONASTERY OF ST. MARY'S HELP,
     GASTON COUNTY, NORTH CAROLINA,
   FEAST OF THE MOST HOLY TRINITY, 1882.

CONFERENCE I.

ON THE EXISTENCE OF THE ONE TRUE GOD.—
THE FATHER, THE FIRST PERSON OF THE
BLESSED TRINITY.

God's Existence a Necessity—If He is not, we are not—The Consent of all Mankind, Reason, Nature, Everything — The Creation of Man—Revelation—No Effect without a Cause—From Nothing Nothing comes—Who is God ?—Chance—Second Causes—Atoms, Numbers—Nonsense—Sad End of Infidels—The Blessed Trinity—One God—Idolatry—Nobility of Man's Origin—God came and spoke to us in the Old and New Testaments—We saw Him, touched Him, and put Him to Death—He arose from the Dead and is with us in the Catholic Church—The Nineteenth Century has greater Motives of Credibility than the First—The Vocation of Abraham —The Law and the Prophets—The Catholic Church a standing Miracle and the Witness—Jesus Christ as God—The Creator and Redeemer—The Light of the World—He is not the God of the Stoics—Thabor and Calvary—Practical Atheism—How is Doubt possible ?—Faith an Act of the Will and Understanding—Not acquired by human Learning—Why are not all learned people Catholic ?—Foe—Plato—Nihilism —The absolute Absurdity—Prayer—Moral Reflections, etc.

I.

I am who am.—Exod. iii. 14.

MY BRETHREN :

You will merit an endless recompense as often as you recite the first article of the Apostles' and Nicene Creeds. They are the formulæ of the faith of the Catholic Church, and by them do we know the fact of God's existence unmixed with error.

"I believe in God, the Father Almighty, Creator of heaven and earth. And of all things visible and invisible." In order to condemn the recent theory of spontaneous production and brutal development, the Holy Ghost, in the Vatican Council, adds, "and in all their substance."

Scientifically we all know that God is; by the virtue of Catholic faith we have the fact on a supernatural basis, in order, as Tertullian remarks, that there may be room for an eternal recompense.

This divine truth is the first known to be written in created language; and justly, because it is the foundation and cause of all religion, civilization, and knowledge, of all that is or can be, and without which nothing can be.

The demonstration of the divine existence is the easiest and the most simple, the greatest and the most essential, act of human reason, which sound philosophy has analyzed, discussed, and confirmed with so much precision and detail for thousands of years that it has attained mathematical certainty, and it is indeed difficult to conceive how a sane man can doubt it.

The denial surpasses in infamy parricide, suicide, or any other crime in the dark roll of immorality. It is Deicide, the fountain of all iniquity. It is a sin against all that exists, for God's cause and His interests are common to all creatures, and the Holy Ghost assures us that the whole universe will avenge their contempt.

We trace the first sad origin of this denial to heaven. The angel through pride rebelled against his bountiful Creator, and was condemned with his forlorn hosts to darkness and endless torments. The once bright leader who shone like the morning star, had nevertheless perverted his intellect by denying, not, indeed, the existence but the rights of his Maker, and was therefore changed into a creeping thing, the most hateful of all brutes. A transformation no less disastrous takes place in the soul of every man who unnaturally, and despite of reason, conscience, and religion, raises his hand against the Most High and in its worst form reasserts the frightful blasphemy. The very name of atheist is so hateful that the impious are ashamed of it and they retain the Holy Name of God while affecting to reject its substance.

God is the Creator and sovereign Lord of

heaven and earth and of all things. He is eternal; He always was and always will be; He had no beginning and will have no end. The great First Cause, he is self-existent, infinite, absolute, free from the limitations and conditions of creatures. He is by the necessity of His being. It is impossible for Him not to be, or otherwise than as He is, with all His infinite perfections and in an adorable Trinity of persons. The Blessed Trinity is God. The divine nature, one and indivisible, is in each Person in its infinite plenitude. He is One, One essentially, and is Oneness itself. He is an unlimited ocean of being and embraces all things within Himself. *In Him we live and move and have our being.* He is a pure spirit, has no body, and makes no impression on our eyes. He sees and knows all things, even our most secret actions and thoughts. He can do all things, and nothing possible can be difficult to Him. He is infinitely good and great, and nothing good can be found in any creature which He does not possess and which does not emanate from Him.

He is the Father of all, and in Him are all paternities in heaven and earth. Every human being, Christian, Jew, Mahometan, or idolater, all are His children, whom He will judge singly, and He will render to every man according to his works. In His sight this world is a speck only in creation. He has made millions of starry worlds ; each of these He could multiply millions of times over, yet He remains unchanged. Let them exceed angelic and human numbers, and they will no more than touch the borders of His infinite power and wisdom.

Such is the testimony of the Catholic Church and her faith from the beginning ; the belief of the synagogue and of the human race since its origin. The creature knows his Author almost by instinct and intuition. The All-Holy revealed Himself to man at the first instant of man's formation ; of a divine necessity the existence of God was in the first thought of man or angel.

If, led by the hand of revelation and reason and in a spirit of prayer, I reverently draw aside the veil of the Sanctuary and exhibit the presence of God in some of His works, my sole object is to increase the love and reverence of my fellow-man for the Father of mercies, who called us out of nothing and bestowed upon us all that we possess. Holy Mary, seat of wisdom, obtain for us by thy prayers light and grace to know and love our Creator and thine, that we may hereafter see and enjoy Him in

His bliss and glory whom we revere and contemplate in His works and especially in our own souls.

There never existed a nation or race of people who did not believe in the existence of God. Throughout the length and breadth of Asia, the cradle-land of the human race and where our civilization had its origin; in mystic Egypt; in Africa; from Malabar to the Bight of Benin; in all the populous cities and along the classic shores of Europe; in this young and yet old America, the secret of creation, like the prophet's hiding-place, from Kane's Sea to the headlands that face the antarctic ice, and among all the coral islands of the ocean, God is known. Civilized or barbarous, the forgotten myriads and the few who have left footprints on the shores of time, all have believed that they were made by Almighty God. Whoever denies this universal conviction is scarcely sane and should be sent for safe-keeping to one of our lunatic asylums. "Tell me," said an English sceptic, to an Arab chief, "how do you know there is a God?" The 'child of the desert, astonished, answered: "Does the sun want light to show himself?"

The opposition of China and Japan to our missionaries; the persecutions of Rome, and

Greece, and Persia, and of all unchristianized nations, which deluged the world with the blood of Christian people, had no other grounds, and claimed no other, than that Catholicity was impious, opposed to the worship of the gods, and that it denied religion.

The universal consent of all nations on any given point is conceded to be the voice of nature and the demonstration of truth. This universal persuasion, anterior to all reflection, undeniably establishes the existence of the one great and merciful God revealing Himself to every child of Adam and *enlightening every man that cometh into this world* (John i.)

In the lapse of time, and as our ancestors removed further away from the fountain of original truth and teachings, the notions of the people became less distinct and their ideas began to differ in regard to the nature and attributes of God. But they were nevertheless in accord on one point—His existence—and it is in proof of this that I invoke their universal assent.

Blinded by their passions or seduced by a false literature, I know not which, some desperate men, to the horror of the world, have made profession of this vast impiety—though, thank God! little known in America—with what degree of sincerity I know not; but their acts refute their notions. They profess honor, justice, truth, all virtues, and affect to keep God's laws while denying that there is a God! Free-thinkers are generally free-livers, and, if I may say so, free-lovers. They are like the persecutors of the Church: their last end is frightful—like beacon-lights warning the world that their approach is dangerous and their contact death. We are all very brave until we are tried. Adversity is the test of sincerity. In the sorrows which come to us all, and at the dread moment of death, they call on God sincerely, whom they despised in their prosperity and in the sunshine of His favors. Some, like the philosopher of Ferney, gather the shattered strength of the spirit into one wild and desperate effort, curse, and die!

Holy Writ declares *that the heavens show forth the glory of God, and the firmament declareth the work of His hands* (Ps. xviii. 1). In the shining pages of this golden book all mankind—the saint and the sinner, the savage and the sage—may read as they run the existence of the Creator and many of His perfections. An admirable plan, a harmony, and an order prevail throughout, adapting with ineffable fitness the means to their proper end and purpose, and displaying infinite wisdom. Who that has any claim to common sense will assert that there can be an effect without a cause, or that nothing can produce something?

If such a person has not quite lost his senses I call his attention to a watch and to its complicated workmanship, and to the fact that each separate piece performs a distinct function, and that all combine to produce the desired effect —that is, to tell the daily hours, minutes, and seconds. He admits it is remarkable, but—it happens by chance.

I accompany him to St. Peter's in Rome, "sole temple worthy of God"; its dimensions, its ornaments, the plan and the materials, like the pyramid of Cheops, are the wonder of the world. He tells me it all happened by chance! I now inform him that the world is spherical and many thousand miles in circumference; that it has two motions—one the diurnal, by which it revolves on its axis a thousand miles an hour in an easterly direction, causing the wonderful succession of day and night; the other its annual motion in its orbit round the sun, in which it speeds with a velocity of sixty-eight thousand miles an hour, producing the wonderful variety of seasons, making the earth the vestibule of heaven were it not for our sins. I prove to him that this motion is so uniform that from the day of creation until now there has not been one moment's difference in the length of the days and the years. Well, it all happened by chance! Merciful God, how less than human are all who forsake thee! Such, you reply, is the extreme of folly; the watch must have had a maker, St. Peter's an architect, and the world a creator.

The goodness, power, and wisdom of our gracious God are everywhere conspicuous. We ought to be grateful to Him, for He has given us our being and all this fair creation as our own to enjoy and possess. He has bestowed upon us a body and soul; He has given us eyes to see, ears to hear, hands to labor, feet to walk, a tongue to speak, a heart to feel. He made the sun to give us light by day, the moon and the stars by night, the yearly harvest to bring forth every variety of fruit pleasing to the eye and pleasant to the taste. He has created all things for the preservation and happiness of His children. We cannot name the thing bright and good within us, nor delectable and attractive without, but it came from our benignant Creator. Cold and less than human, then, must the heart be that will not glow with love and gratitude towards Him.

Throughout the vast expanse of the universe
there is not an object, not an atom, that does
not wear the imprint, the seal and signet, of an
all-wise Intelligence. The humblest flower of
the vale, the meekest shrub by brook or
fountain, the tiniest insect, the beasts of the
field, the birds of the air, the fish of the sea—
land, sea, and sky themselves—everything, great
and small, bears the same ineffaceable trace of
their Maker and of the Triune God.

Everything is in an incessant motion. It is
like a universal soul of creation and could
proceed but from an infinitely wise and omnipotent cause. This is one of the powerful arguments of St. Thomas in proof of the divine
existence.

I speak not of the lesser motions of men
and animals, nor of those produced by them
or by secondary causes, but of the mysterious
motion of the earth round its axis and in its
orbit, of the whole planetary system, of the
ponderous orbs in the nightly heavens, of the
motion of the entire universe round some unknown centre in the realms of space, perhaps
the very throne of God, before which all the
sanctities of heaven stand in profound adoration. All things set in towards Him in an irresistible tide. The earth, the solar system,

2

all matter, is essentially inert, and would for
ever remain so were they not impelled into mo·
tion by an external and co-efficient cause, who
can only be the Lord of the universe, Himself
immutable and external. *He measured the waters in the hollow of His hand, and weighed
the mountains in scales,* and *with three fingers
poised the bulk of the earth* (Isa. xl.)

The creation of man undoubtedly establishes
the same fact. He did not always live on
earth. The annals of time and all historical
monuments give him a duration not more remote than nearly six thousand years. Fossil
remains lead to the same conclusion. Man
could not have existed from eternity, for the
world itself is not eternal. If he has always
lived how has it happened that, with all his
skill, energy, and restless ambition, he has
left no trace, no monument of His labors of a
greater age than that I have indicated?

An infinite succession of created beings is
an absurdity, like the theories of atoms and
numbers. The number of the links in such a
succession must be infinite and at the same
time limited—infinite in the supposition of an
eternal succession, and yet not so because of
its daily increment. Numbers can add nothing
to infinity, for infinity contains all in itself.

Atoms also are an absurdity; they should have created themselves, or have acted before they existed, which would of course be a little too soon.

Man, then, having a beginning, could be made only by the Almighty, who fashioned him to His own image and likeness. He is like God in being a spirit and immortal as to his soul, and in being capable of knowing and loving Him. Taking pity on us, God called us from nothing in preference to others who are in the abyss of the divine possibility. Our likeness lived in His mind from eternity. All we are or have is His; our creation is our share in His infinite goodness. Surely we should adore, love, and serve Him.

Reason is a ray of the divine mind and generally reliable within its own legitimate province—the natural order. Its powers are amazing, and man is overwhelmed at its varied developments. But it is too feeble to penetrate into the mysteries of God. Yet God sheds upon it the brightness of His light, both in the Old and the New Testament, and their combined splendors lead us into all truth. The full deposit of divine revelation is preserved pure and unalterable in the Catholic Church, and parts of it are contained in both Testaments, of the veracity, integrity, authenticity, and inspiration of which she is the infallible and living witness. She makes God more clearly known than does unaided human reason. He came visibly into this world and spoke to the human race face to face. The powers of the heavens are amazed and all rational beings astonished at His infinite condescension; His excessive goodness is even a temptation. He has spoken, not merely by an angel, a prophet, or celestial envoy, but in His own person: the Father, the Son, and the Holy Ghost each has conversed with us here on earth. God has even become man and has assumed our very nature.

After the dispersion of the race of Adam from the plains of Sennaar men ignored the unity of God and fell into idolatry. They worshipped a plurality of gods. They were ignorant of His nature and attributes; they idolized themselves and everything else except the one true God. Even sins had statues and were publicly adored with incense and sacrifice, as they are to-day, in heart, by millions of civilized people. Ambition, gold and lust, and all other vices are still the popular divinities. Darkness and the shadow of death passed over the world like a shoreless ocean. Yet all believed in God without being able to tell who

or what He was, remarked one of their sages.
The men renowned for learning in these ancient times established an independent FIRST
CAUSE, cold and indifferent to His works and
as unsympathetic as Athos or Atlas.
A new light bursts through the universal
gloom. "Let all nations rejoice, let the hills
and mountains, let the cedars of Lebanon rejoice; let all beasts and cattle and all things be
exceeding glad; for the Lord has visited the
earth, and His children shall no more abide in
darkness nor pine beneath the cold shades of
death."

Our relations are explained. The Almighty
is our Father and we are His children. All paternities combined cannot equal His love for
His every child. He is our friend—the only
friend we have on earth; our lover—all other
loves are but a fancy; He is our Creator, and
that implies all. We can converse with Him
and are united with Him by faith, hope, and
charity.

In the book of Genesis, the first annals of
time, we read that God created heaven and
earth for man's use and benefit; that He fashioned man's body from the slime of the earth
and breathed into him an immortal soul, a
spark of His own being, one of His own im-

perishable thoughts, and made him the lord of
creation—of the birds of the air, the beasts of
the field, the fishes of the sea. All things were
made subject to man, and he was subject to
God only. How noble is man's origin, how
more than regal, how God-like! He is a supernatural being, who believes in God, adores
Him, trusts in Him, and loves Him.

In after-times God makes an alliance with
Abraham, one of our race, and promises that his
offspring shall outnumber the stars of heaven,
on one condition—that they believe in Him and
keep His commandments. The covenant is renewed to Isaac and to Jacob. This knowledge
of the one true God was never lost among this
people. When about to be gathered to his
fathers the dying patriarch Jacob imparted a
prophetic blessing on each of his sons, and
spake in this manner to Juda: *Juda, thee
shall thy brethren praise; the sceptre shall not
be taken away from Juda, nor a ruler from
his thigh, till He come that is to be sent,
and He shall be the expectation of nations*
(Gen. xlix. 10). This faith never perished, but
always lived with the Jews, whether in the
brick-fields of Egypt, on the burning sands of
the desert, under the impious kings, under the
harsh schism of Samaria, in proud Babylon or

in gorgeous Ninive. It outlived the hot persecutions of the Syrian monarchs, and remained pure until Jesus Christ came into the world.

II.

In the desert Moses is commissioned from on high to conduct the children of Israel from the slavery of Egypt to the land of promise, and that passage from Egypt to the land of promise is a type and a prophecy of our present condition and our future hopes. The meek son of Amram asked God His name, and He answered (Exod. iii., etc.) : "I AM WHO AM. Thus shalt thou say to the children of Israel : HE WHO IS hath sent me to you." And Moses was commissioned to tell his people : Thou shalt have no strange gods before me ; thou shalt not take the name of the Lord thy God in vain ; remember to keep holy the Sabbath day ; honor thy father and thy mother ; thou shalt not kill ; thou shalt not commit adultery ; thou shalt not steal ; thou shalt not lie ; thou shalt not covet thy neighbor's wife ; thou shalt not covet thy neighbor's goods.

Three thousand years have elapsed since God gave these commandments to mankind through the ministry of Moses, and they remain unaltered to the present day; they never will be changed, for they are founded on the relation of the Creator to His rational creature—man. They are superior to every other code in wisdom and sanctity. In a merely human sense they have made Moses superior to Solon, to Lycurgus, and to all other legislators, and the Jewish nation greater in wisdom and knowledge than all the sages of Greece and Rome.

The philosophers believed in God, but they could not tell who or what He was nor how He must be worshipped; they were ignorant of His nature and attributes. Now Moses said: *Hear, O Israel! the Lord thy God is one Lord; thou shalt love the Lord thy God with thy whole heart and with thy whole soul, with thy whole strength* (Deut.) In the Psalms especially does God manifest Himself more openly and plainly; His inward life is disclosed, His precepts and our obligations inculcated; His name is in every verse, implicitly or expressly; the prayers are expressive of every sentiment of piety and devotion that can animate the heart of man. The first Psalm declares him blessed who fears the Lord, and the last invites all nations to praise and bless His holy name.

As in nature everything has a tongue to speak of God, so also in Holy Writ, but more distinctly. There is not a verse, nor an event, nor a miracle, nor a prophecy in the Bible which does not prove His all-holy being, directly or indirectly. The Old Testament is the prophecy of the New. All its contents wear their face to the dawn and rising of the Sun of Justice. Many centuries before the birth of Christ, Isaias foretold that Jerusalem would be enlightened with a great light ; that all nations would come from afar to unite themselves with Israel. The inhabitants of Madian would come with camels, and those of Saba would bring their gold and incense. All the nations of the earth would unite as one in paying homage to Emmanuel—God in human flesh. Zacharias, filled with the Holy Ghost, announces *that God has visited the earth, the Orient from on high, to enlighten those who sit in darkness and in the shadow of death.* St. John the Baptist, this voice crying in the wilderness, declares on the banks of the Jordan that he is not himself the Light, but the witness thereof, to bear testimony that there stands in their midst the One who enlightens every man that cometh into the world.

Christ appears after having been announced for four thousand years by an unbroken line of prophets, expected by all the just, prefigured by all rites and ceremonies, and typified by

3

all the sacrifices of the true religion. All nations longed for Him, all ages sighed for Him.
The prophets of the gentiles gazed from afar
on the star of Jacob, and the oracles of the
idols at Delphi and at the fountains of Egeria
proclaimed His advent. He was hailed as the
legislator of all ages, the light of all nations,
and the salvation of the universe.

His every word and act, the manner of His
birth, its circumstances, all the events of His
life, Thabor and Calvary, the sepulchre and
Olivet, proved Him to be God. His is the name
of essence, I AM. His is identity of nature and
works with the Father, for *the Father and He
are one* and the same God. He is the supreme
Lord of the living and the dead.

He delivers an oracle which none before nor
since could utter : *I am the light of the
world; he who followeth me walketh not in
darkness.* He spake in this manner because,
outside of Jerusalem, all the world was buried
in darkness and vice. It was the Augustan
age, the golden age of learning, science, and
art. Reason had achieved its greatest victo-
ries ; sculpture, painting, architecture, oratory,
poetry—all sciences and arts, had unveiled
their splendors and irradiated the known
world from pole to pole. Yet never before

had mankind been so corrupt. Virtue was only a name and a shame. Every degrading vice was worshipped as a god. Every species of vice was attributed to the ever-blessed Sanctity of heaven. While God's existence was acknowledged His nature, His perfections, and His name were unknown. His disciples for three centuries, and up to this day in pagan countries, were tortured to death.

Now, as formerly, human learning does not render men good and virtuous. Without God it only serves to make men slaves to error and to refine and intensify their passions. One of those ancient sages remarked that so deplorable was the moral condition of the world that God Himself must needs come and redress it or it must perish. Justly, then, did God say, *I am the light of the world;* and in his Epistles to the Thessalonians St. Paul styles the believers *children of light.*

Standing before the august council of the Areopagus, the Apostle of the Gentiles announces the most startling truth that ever fell on their ears: "Ye men of Athens, I perceive that in all things you are too superstitious. For passing by and seeing your idols, I found an altar on which was written, *To the unknown God.* What therefore you worship, without knowing it, that I preach to you : God, who made the world and all things therein, seeing He is Lord of heaven and earth. . . . It is He who giveth to all life and breath, and all things. . . . In Him we live, and move, and are ; as some also of your own poets said : *For we are also His offspring.*"

The apostles are sent to announce the gospel of truth, the full-orbed revelation, to all the nations of the earth. And their teachings are perpetuated in the Catholic Church, the infallible and divinely constituted organ of all truth, co-extensive with the universe, which will last to the end of the world. The Church is the living witness of the existence of her divine Founder, the one true God, and of all His perfections. He who knowingly rejects her doctrines will be lost. He who does not believe her would not believe one from the dead. Endure she must while virtue is an obligation, while a soul is to be saved, and while God is to be honored and believed on earth. Her earthly reign will only terminate when the myriads who slumber in the dust, clothed in their proper flesh, shall stand before the tribunal of Jesus Christ to receive every one according to his works.

Countless hosts of all nations and tongues

adore in spirit and in truth the one true God. Zealous missionary bishops and priests carry His name to distant shores and reclaim their less favored inhabitants from idolatry and consequent vice, and bring them into this admirable light. Holy pontiffs, religious men and women innumerable, form the tenor of their actions and lives according to the maxims of the Uncreated Truth ; millions of martyrs have died to witness it, and almost all the great and learned of ancient and Christian times have illustrated it by their writings.

Every truth is one in itself and also in the relation it holds towards all others pertaining to the system to which it belongs, whether in the material, the intellectual, or the supernatural kingdom. They all emanate from God, who is truth essential, embracing them in an admirable simplicity.

As God is necessarily His own end in all His works, in like manner is He His own type and model. The more perfect the work the closer the resemblance. The soul is more like God than the body, and the Church than material creation, its groundwork. The essential marks of the Church, her doctrines and mysteries, are combined in an admirable unity and under one head, like the perfections in the divine simplicity. All our Lord's works expressed this similitude to His attributes. The manner in which He came and dwelt amongst us is like unto His unknown life, which fills us with awe and wonder. Without a revelation an archangel even could not imagine that the full face of God would be turned to the world, not from Sinai but from the cross and between two thieves, in the midst of a reviling mob. Always like Himself, as at the beginning so now also it is from darkness that light is called to illumine the moral waste.

In its nature every sin is a rebellion, high treason, and an attempt against God's existence; though it be not formal atheism, it implies atheism. Hence sinners are styled the ungodly.

In modern society there are found three classes of infidels or atheists, and their number is alarming. The first are the free-thinkers, who, while retaining the name of God, like the heathens of old, deny His nature and His divine perfections. Pantheists are prominent under this disastrous classification. Their God is a grand total, not perfect but in progress; not a person, for he is not conscious and knows himself but in the fragment of humanity; not

a love, but blindly impelled by the laws of
nature; without will, liberty, or unlimited intellect—the God of the Stoics.

. The second class embraces all the atheists,
who deny God in His images and in the persons and things that specially represent Him
—all who are averse to religion; and their
number is vast. God came in human flesh;
they reject him. God is in His Church, which
is the tabernacle of the Real Presence, the organ of the Holy Ghost, the witness of all
truth. God is in the pope, who is the successor of St. Peter, the visible head of the
Church, the vicar of Christ, the witness and
the infallible assertion of God. The war of
nearly all nations to-day is universal and desperate against the Church, against the Lord
and His anointed. Governments nominally Catholic persecute Catholicity intensely with sa-
tanic hatred, and her august head has not a
spot on earth on which he may rest. God is
in man, because man is made to God's image
and likeness and bears on his brow the light
of God's face (Ps. iv. 7). Schools of modern
philosophy in the most civilized communities
have sacrilegiously torn the diadem of immortality from man's head and they style him an
improved specimen of a brute. How true is the

word of God! When, in opposition to the divine mandate, man makes to himself a false
God, like Satan or Nabuchodonosor, he bé-
comes like unto the works of his hands, a sense-
less animal (Ps. cxiii. 16). God is in His priests,
in the religious orders, and in the religious life.
Who are more despised and depreciated? God
is in His word, in the faith, and in all virtues :
And the Word was God. This, it is true, is all
denied ; people may now become saints without
the grace of God and contrary to the model of
Jesus Christ, in despite of Him and without His
grace. God is in the marriage bond, the fountain of the human race, whose waters must be
preserved pure and limpid. But this tie is now
a rope of sand. God is in civilization. Now,
these insane enemies of all truth assert that
civilization is merely a natural evolution of
progress ; and they teach, at the end of nineteen centuries enlightened by our Lord, that
our Lord is an obstacle and must needs be
removed.

These pestilential teachings are spread far
and wide; they are the natural result of heresies, and they have poisoned all the fountains
of education, have banished God from the domain of science, and have caused countless
numbers to suffer shipwreck of their faith.

The third class embraces the practical atheists—those who believe in God, but deny Him in act and violate His commandments. They are innumerable and are in all professions and denominations. Temptations are strong and varied ; we have free-will, and nature is frail. But there are crimes of great malignity which shock and terrify society—such, for example, as when a priest falls or becomes "an atheist at the altar of God." Without being intended for a formal denial of the existence of God, all sins naturally tend to this frightful abyss, for after the first step from the path of rectitude, without speedy repentance, no man can tell where the end will be.

With evidences so convincing, it is asked, how it is possible for a sane person to doubt the existence of God, who is the necessary object of the mind, as light is of the eye? Without contact with Him man's mind could no more conceive a thought than his hand could create a world. First, because they do not wish to believe and every man can reject the grace of faith. True belief in the existence of God is not derived from human learning nor from philosophy ; otherwise all the renowned scholars of ancient and modern times would have been Catholic.

The heart is the nearest road to heaven. *Blessed are the clean of heart, for they shall see God* (Matt. v. 8). When the will refuses its assent the understanding cannot perfect its act ; yet faith is the result, with the assistance of grace, of the combined co-operation of both faculties. There can, it is true, be a sterile and abstract conviction, for conviction does not necessarily induce practice ; if it did nearly all men would be virtuous.

Secondly, truth and error, or virtue and vice, which are synonymous for affirmation and negation, are the two extremes of human life ; the perilous choice comes daily to every man, and, by a law of his nature, he is necessitated to make it. The just choose the real, the substantial, the true, which unite them more closely to God. The unjust pursue an opposite course : they make choice of avarice, sensuality, or other passion, which they make their god. It is a new phase of old paganism. In all this there is nothing real, for every sin is a lie. Habituated to prefer the unreal, the false, and the things that are not, to the real and true, selfishness is their idol, and they end in believing nothing. Faith and morals go hand-in-hand and sustain one another.

In this country the denial of God is seldom

formal. But though possessing many social
qualities, the masses of the people are growing more indifferent, and they seldom give God,
their salvation, or the future a serious thought.
They conform to some easy form of public
worship which imposes no real obligation.
Their state is one rather of a good-natured religious indifference than of direct negation of
the Almighty God.

Thirdly, atheism is formally professed by
some unhappy people in other countries under
the name of Nihilism. As vice is the result
of perverting the will against the laws of morals, Nihilism consists in turning reason against
itself, perverts its laws, and pretends that Nothing is the principle and cause of all things!

The perfections of all creatures can come
from their Creator only. By overstepping
their limits and extending them to the infinite we obtain an invincible proof of the existence of God. The Nihilists reverse the process; they deny the perfection, push the negation to the infinite, and proclaim that *there
exists* an absolute nothing! This process furnishes us with an astonishing result. Philo-
sophically considered, the theory of atheism is
in spite of itself a vigorous and unassailable
proof, backward or by the reverse course, of

the existence of God, showing that the denial of God's existence leads to an ABSURDITY. This is as it should be; the common sense of the human race, the reasoning of thousands of years, as well as revelation, prove that God exists. Unless right reason stultifies itself, right reason must show the ABSURDITY of the theory that denies it.

These unhappy atheists push their insane notion to an extreme point, and maintain that the principle of contradiction is false, which means that we can affirm and deny the pro and con, the for and against, of everything, at the same time and under the same circumstances; according to their logic it would be true to say that at the same time America exists and does not exist, that virtue and vice, truth and falsehood, right and wrong, are all merely one and the same thing.

These fallacies are as old as the hills; the East is rampant with them; Foe is their accredited author. The sophists of Greece adopted them; they are at the bottom of all those Eastern heresies which assailed the Church, and which were chiefly speculative denials.

But these fallacies are not reasoning; they are mere sophistry, which would lead us to conclude that there is no truth because there

are untruths; that there is no certainty because there are cases of doubt; that we know
nothing because there is some knowledge beyond our reach; and that we should make no
effort because we are not omnipotent. This
sophistry leads its votaries astray from the
plain path of truth, bewilders them in a
labyrinth of error, and then sneers at their
baffled efforts to extricate themselves. Sound
philosophy, on the other hand, lays down
firm premises, concedes truths and axioms, and
draws the irresistible conclusion, leading in a
way in which even fools cannot err.

"Philosophy and sophistry," remarks Plato, "go in opposite directions: one towards
being, and the other towards nothing. And
while philosophy is flooded with the brilliancy
of the light of its object, sophistry is blinded
by its own."

The Holy Ghost assures us that a man is
punished in the things in which he sins. The
grace which he rejects is often withdrawn and
given to others. This fact is illustrated in the
history of individuals and nations.

All the East, the cradle-land of the Gospel,
and many parts of central and western Europe, rejected God and His Church. They are
now falling rapidly into absolute infidelity.

Their material prosperity, their progress, and their literature serve but to blind them the more, and their power is waning. God is the end of His works; the world will last only while it adores Him, and the human race while it continues to give saints for heaven, and no longer. Both failing in these respects, the annals of time close and the end comes.

A correct idea of God gives the proof of His existence in itself and in His works.

Of a necessity the soul seeks being, and in it the Infinite. Every sight and sound and contact with external objects, all our impressions, and the sensations of the soul, should elevate us to God. God is present everywhere. He is really and substantially in every being. I touch God implicitly and *mediately* when I come in contact with any body whatever. He also co-operates with every act and He acts at least permissively in every agent. He is at the root of every thought and in every act of the will. Light, heat, odors, tastes, attractions, emotions, are the effects of the omnipresent Creator and of His contact with all bodies. God causes the sun to give us light, which it could not do without His impulse, and this requires His presence. In every being and in every motion God is present as the efficient prime motive power. When we receive an impression through an object it comes from God as its primary cause. If we possessed sufficient vivacity of sentiment and emotion the soul would with the speed of lightning reach God and embrace Him, the infinite Power which it discovers in itself and in all things besides, and would rest contented in the very being of the Father Almighty. "The whole world," said the pagan poet, "is filled with God." The saints saw God in everything, and the simplest objects threw them into ecstasy. Who, in favored moments, has not felt his very soul thrill with the presence of God through the medium of surrounding creatures?

The consideration of our intimacy with God cannot fail to fill the soul with awe and love. It is in Him, indeed, that we live; all our thoughts, words, and actions are written in the book of life, which is the being of the everlasting God Himself. The blood of our Lord will wash away from the soul of the penitent sinner every stain of sin and make it whiter than snow. But never will it remove the remembrance of the transgression from the divine Mind ; that remembrance will endure after Time itself shall have spent his course. Woe, then, to him who falls unprepared into the hands of

the living God! Better for him that he had
never been born than have lived in vain and
have denied the Lord who made him.

The prayer rightly offered, the temptation resisted, the injury forgiven, and the cross meek-
ly borne are facts firm as the throne of God,
and their recompense will be greater than their
duration. It will be no single gift or attribute,
but God whole and entire—God possessed and
all our own.

Pride can never learn anything about God ;
on the contrary, it has failed in all its efforts.
Humble prayer is the universal grace of all
men, and it will surely bring conviction, for it
is the seed of faith. *If any of you want wisdom let him ask of God, who giveth to all
abundantly and upbraideth not: and it shall
be given him* (James i. 5).

Every relation in which the divine Majesty
stands towards us furnishes constraining motives of daily beginning love and service. We
have duties towards Him, towards ourselves and
our neighbor. All these are contained in the
golden precept, which is of universal obligation
—the love of God and of our neighbor.

In the case of blameless ignorance salvation
is possible beyond the visible pale of the
Church. But it is impossible for any human

being, of whatsoever state or condition, to be saved unless he loves God above all things, and his neighbor as himself, according to the measure of his light and grace. God's love for each of us surpasses the power of imagination, and perhaps measures the divine possibilities; for He asks by the mouth of the prophet Isaias: *What more can I do for my vineyard that I have not done?* He not only demands our love, but merits it because of what He has done for us, and because of the excellence of His nature and perfections. He cannot but be desirable to all intelligent beings because of His infinite beauty, goodness, and love. If but a single drop of the sweetness of His goodness fell on the hopeless regions of the lost it would extinguish all its flames and change it into paradise in an instant. His power is omnipotent; nothing is difficult to Him; His duration is eternity; His home is immensity; His measure is infinity, and His course is unchangeable. *His treasures have no end* (Is. ii. 7). *He has fixed all things in measure, number, and weight* (Wisd. xi. 2). *He is high in His strength, and none is like Him* (Job xxxvi. 22). *He is higher than heaven, and what wilt thou do? He is deeper than hell, and how wilt thou know? The measure of Him is longer than*

4

the earth, is broader than the sea (Job xii. 8, 9). *In whose hand is the soul of every living thing and the spirit of all flesh of man* (Job xii. 10). *Whose wrath no man can resist, and under whom they stoop that bear up the world* (Job ix. 13). *Thousands of thousands ministered to Him, and ten thousand times a hundred thousand stood before Him* (Dan. vii. 10). *Who is able to declare His works? Who shall search out His glorious acts? Who shall show forth the power of His majesty?* (Ecclus. xviii. 2 et seq.)

Because of the nature of His love for us, and because of His infinite perfections, we should in return love Him and keep His commandments, *and they are not heavy.* Let us thank the Father of mercies, *who has called us out of darkness into His marvellous light* (1 Peter ii. 9). Let us pray for those who are in the darkness of infidelity, that they, too, may know and serve Him here on earth and reign with Him in Heaven.

Now, *To the King of ages, immortal and invisible, the only God, be honor and glory for ever and ever. Amen* (1 Tim. i. 17).

CONFERENCE II.

ON THE DIVINE PERFECTIONS, ALL TOTALLY POSSESSED BY EACH PERSON OF THE MOST HOLY TRINITY.

Other Proofs of the Existence of the Most High—All holy and honorable Names are His Attributes—The Name of Essence —The divine Nature and Attributes the same—All deduced from one as a Premise—Essential and moral Attributes— Unimaginable Life of God—Eternity and Immensity correlative—Nothing from Nothing proceeds—Immutability— Unity and Simplicity—All God's Attributes and Perfections are one—Justly distinguished in our Conceptions—St. Irenæus—The divine Essence never seen by mortal Man—Incomprehensible—Moral Attributes pertain to God as Creator —Permission of Evil—God is not the Author of Sin—Wisdom—Knowledge, but not Foreknowledge—Love, Truth, Mercy, Justice—Alpha and Omega—Man's limited Perfections prove the Infinite—Moral Reflections, etc., etc.

I.

He who is (EXOD. iii. 14).

MY BRETHREN:

When I last addressed you I proved that heaven and earth and the vast expanse of creation established the existence of the great First Cause, and that man's creation, his every thought, word, and act, and the laws of universal motion, confirmed THE ETERNAL ACT. I also explained how reason and religion vindicated the truth with mathematical certainty, and that all arguments combined produced the general persuasion of mankind—an unerring test of truth. Permit me now to remark that, even if engaged in the occupation for eternity, neither angels nor men could fathom a single attribute of God or exhaust the evidences of His existence. This truth should be borne in mind, lest perhaps the paltry efforts of man in this direction serve but to dishonor and lower the Great Supreme in our estimation. If a seraph could totally understand God he would by that fact cease to be a creature.

This universal conviction from which no race has escaped is a necessity of the human mind; His evidences are implanted in the soul by the hand of the omnipotent Creator, which no sophistry can eliminate, no passion destroy; the passions may burn out all traces of virtue and goodness besides, and leave the moral empire a ruin and a wreck.

The adorable, self-sufficient essence of the Most High God has been established by the most learned that ever have lived, on the same grounds from which the gentiles derived the

roots of moral obligations and the entire race
of man all their axioms and first principles
of common sense and rectitude, and where
sound philosophy and moral theology, in a
measure, have discovered their majors and the
incontestable principles of truth—the fact of
creation and the innate conviction and intuition of the soul.

These convictions are anterior to the process
of reasoning. They flash on the mind with a
persuasion greater than can be derived from
any process of argumentation, for they are the
groundwork itself of argumentation and the
materials of philosophy. That I live, that I
am bathed in a flood of light, that I was created by the sovereign Lord of the universe, are
facts which I believe with a conviction that
even all the philosophical reasoning of Plato or
St. Thomas could not produce. They are the
innate convictions of the immortal soul. This
is the conviction with which all men are persuaded that God exists.

St. Paul affirms that so plainly is the Almighty God manifested in His works that we
are inexcusable if we do not know the invisible from the things that are seen. It is as
unreasonable to deny Him as it is to deny our
own existence or that of the world. Hence

theologians deny the possibility of blameless ignorance regarding a fact so incontestably established by creation, by reason, by revelation, by the senses, by innate conviction. In regard to the certainty of this eternal truth our condition differs from that of the just in heaven in this: that they behold Him face to face, whereas we see Him indirectly or mediately through the light of reason and of faith.

It is by His attributes that God is known; they are His nature.

The errors of mankind have been concerning God's nature rather than His existence. The great evil and misfortune of men is the ignoring of the rights of the Creator. This is indeed the sad mystery of human perversity. Practically there is scarcely another truth so little realized, and there are none more out of place than is God in His own world, or whom men so persistently forget; the bare remembrance of Him is an excellence.

When men by their vices and errors had clouded the great truth He threw an additional flood of light around it, that it might be more distinctly understood and that the obligations it imposes might be more faithfully observed. In the solitude of the wilderness He revealed

Himself to the Hebrew legislator by a new name, the name of essence, which measures the plenitude of His existence, expresses all the divine nature and His infinite perfections, and to which nothing could be added, for it contains eminently and without limitation the excellences of all beings, actual and possible. "I AM WHO I AM. Thus shalt thou say to the children of Israel: HE WHO IS, SENT ME" (Exod. iii. 14. Thus He distinctly teaches us who He is and what is His nature; that He is living, absolute, self-existing, and necessary; that He exists by necessity and is life itself—not merely a condition or accidental quality of it, but His essence and nature; that without Him nothing can be; that all things exist in Him and from Him and by Him (Rom. xi. 36).

St. John of Damascus appropriately remarks: "He who is, is God's first and greatest name, for He embraces all things in Himself, and He possesses existence itself, the infinite ocean of being. He is called life because he is its fountain. *I live*, saith the Lord (Jer. xxii. 24). *He gives life to all* (Acts xvii. 25). He hath life in Himself (John v. 26). Being is his essential name, glorious, incommunicable, ineffable. It expresses all that God is. Wonderful name! who dare profane it? Gleaming on Aaron's

breastplate, only the high-priest must speak
it."

Pantheism, in asserting that all things are
God, as implicitly denies God as the Nihilists,
who say that nothing is God. For the incessant changes of things show that they are not
necessary, while their discord, one neutralizing
the other, proves that they have not an identity
of substance. A succession of secondary causes
is no less ridiculous, for they are not all intelligent, and the first link must have made itself! A being infinitely wise and powerful, by
whom all these things were made, must be distinct from them.

Holy Writ says that *God is in all things*
(Ecclus. xliii. 29). *All things were made by His
word; He is omnipotent above all His works*
(ibid. 30). The origin and preservation of
all things are ascribed to Him. *He is great
and has no end, high and immense* (Baruch iii.
25). We receive from Him life and motion,
but not His divine nature (Rom. xi. 5). Therefore all things were created by Him, nor can
there be a perfection in any creature which
does not exist in God eminently and in a different manner.

Reason, revelation, and innate conviction
prove that there is one, and only one, God, the

infinitely perfect Being. A fact thus established, and confirmed by the universal assent of mankind and with mathematical certainty, becomes a fixed principle from which as a premise all the divine attributes are derived and follow one after another as a logical induction. In possession of one attribute, reason draws all the others from the first by way of syllogism, just as we deduce in algebra all that the given formula implies. This order is followed by St. Thomas. He first proves the existence of God by motion. According to the inductive system, which grants the major, he proves the prime motive power to be immutable. Taking immutability as one of God's metaphysical perfections, he deduces from it step by step and in an unbroken chain the divine attributes.

God's attributes are his perfections; they are His nature and the conditions of His being. Eternity, infinity, immensity, immutability, omnipotence, wisdom, perfection, and holiness—these eight are essential. They contain the inmost life of the Great Supreme, independent of His external works. They are the conditions of his essence and of all we attribute to it, and belong to the self-sufficiency of God separately from creation. There are six others, making fourteen in all, touching His relation

5

to external things or creatures. These six are dominion, providence, benevolence, justice, mercy, love, as well as His being the beginning and end of all things.

Although creation is not eternal, it always existed in the divine Mind from everlasting, and hence God was never absolutely without His works. They are in Him eminently and without the limits of creatures, and more perfectly; for their conceptions are eternal and immutable. The work of the artist does not essentially alter his nature; much less can God be changed by his outward works. The foreseen worship of His creatures was the same before God always that it is now and in act.

Yet we may consider God, the august Trinity, in the threefoldness of persons and in the unity of essence, in the abstract or without creatures. His eternal solitude is a conception that overwhelms the mind with awe, self-sufficing; He is His own glory, His own greatness, His own love, His own infinite beatitude, His own interminable life. Let Him multiply new systems for every orb now in existence, and there will remain unexplored the infinite residence of His unknown and unimaginable life.

The All-Holy Lord, self-existing and absolute, or free from the conditions of creatures, must necessarily be infinite—not at one point, but on all sides and in every possible way and manner. A limited being exists to a certain point only, and there it dies; it does not exist beyond it, like regal authority beyond its own proper state. Such a being is circumscribed and limited by qualifications and fixed boundaries. He is not simple and absolute— not the infinite I AM WHO AM.

We are so saturated with creatures that we think of the Uncreated Majesty as a creature under a creature's form and transfer to Him their image. But the mind must needs soar above these habitual distractions and fix its steady gaze on the divine simplicity. If the Creator were restricted in any sense or at any point he could not be or exist beyond that point, nor could he be at all. Infinite in essence and in every manner, this incomprehensible perfection qualifies all His attributes. He is not only infinitely patient and compassionate, but he is infinity itself. It may be styled His sole perfection, because it includes all. It is frequently inculcated in Holy Scripture: The Lord *is great and hath no end; He is high and immense* (Baruch iii. 25). *His greatness has no end* (Ps. xliv. 3).

Some divines maintain that numerically God's attributes cannot be counted. All honorable and magnificent terms can be applied to Him and are His predicates. Whatever perfection is found in the creature is but a quality of the plenitude thereof in God. His adorable, self-subsisting essence combines all, not only in their various degrees, but eminently and without any of the limits and privations that attend them in creatures. Thus He is not only good but goodness, not only holy but holiness. He enjoys all things in an infinite manner; and, in the opinion of some theologians, their number surpasses created conception and can be known only to Himself. He possesses them in an absolute simplicity which belongs only to God. The brightness of the light around His throne is so intense as to be inaccessible, and is called darkness in Holy Writ. Because He is ineffable, silence seems His meetest praise. The saints were mostly speechless during their ecstasies.

Existing by the necessity of His nature, it is obvious even to reason alone that Jehovah must be infinite in every sense. It therefore follows, as a necessary consequence of this fact, that He is all that is possible. Because if not in this sense and under this condition, there

would be a limit beyond which He would not
exist; or, what is equivalent, there would be
no God at all, if He were not infinitely all
that is possible. He is not only all that is
possible, but possibility and act are one and
inseparable in Him. *He doeth all things
whatsoever He willeth, in heaven and on
earth* (Ps. ciii.) One of the Fathers remarks what is most true but truly wonderful: "That, being a simple act, God exercises
His omnipotence in order to do nothing." All
possibilities are actual in Him. It is by His
omnipotence that He did not create sooner or
differently. Yet in the presence of eternity
there is no period of time, sooner or later. Immensity and eternity are correlative attributes
with infinity. For by the very same reason
for which God is infinite He must be immense
and eternal. If not eternal, then there was a
time when He was not; and if not immense,
there is a place in which He is not. In such
a case, then, He would not be pure, simple,
and absolute being; there, in fact, would be
no God at all. God is present everywhere, especially in heaven, where He manifests Himself
to the blessed. He is in the soul of the saint
and in the spirit of evil, in all His infinite being, and the difference is in the different man-

ner in which He communicates Himself—not the same way in any two individuals.

The question why anything exists is absurd. Because God necessarily is it is impossible for Him not to exist in all places and at all times. There never was an alternative between being and no being, between something and nothing. There never was a time when the All-Holy Majesty did not exist and as He is now. There never was and never can be a possibility of His not being. It is a divine necessity, and here he is not free; this is a perfection of His nature. It is as impossible that God should not have existed as it is impossible that nothing ever existed, that nothing was or ever could be.

Both propositions are contradictory and mutually destroy one another. The following propositions are identical and express the same idea. Being exists, and nothing does not exist. From nothing nothing ever could come. The Supreme Being exists, and exists necessarily. No doubt of this could arise except in the instance of one who has not a correct idea of the great First Cause, self-existing and necessary.

God must be of Himself, otherwise He must have proceeded from another; in which case He would not be absolute, but secondary and relative, and that other would be God, which is absurd. Therefore if the Almighty God is necessary He must be of Himself. But this is merely the same idea in two forms.

II.

It is strictly true that because God, who created us, is eternal and immense He must be simultaneously in all places and at every point of time. We can form some idea of His ubiquity, or presence in every point of space, but to conceive how He can be present at every point of time baffles human understanding. Yet, being absolute, He must needs be present simultaneously at all points both of space and time. All past ages are present to Him. In His presence there is no past nor future, but an unsuccessive, unchanging now. Time and space are man's home temporarily. The past, the present, and the future are the knowledge of God, and are embraced by His infinity and in its ineffable simplicity. All periods of time meet in Him as a unit, as all lines drawn from the circumference of a circle meet in the centre.

Unaided reason proves that the Necessary Being is eternal, without beginning, end, or succession ; that He always was, for it is impossi-

ble to conceive how He could spring from nothing. "If ever," said a philosopher and a
Christian, "there was an instant when there
was nothing, nothing should last for ever."
There would be nothing now. *I am the first
and the last*, says the Lord (Isa. xli. 1). He is
the ALPHA AND THE OMEGA of the Apocalypse.

Eternity is the simultaneous and perfect possession of an interminable life. The long and
weary lapse of indefinite ages compared to it
is less than the raindrop to the ocean. How
ineffable the bliss that gathers into every
moment, into every thought, the accumulated
joys of infinite perfections and beatitudes!

The Holy Ghost frequently proclaims the immensity of God. He is whole and entire everywhere and in everything, in every being, not
more in the angel than in the insect, not more
in the orb of the firmament than in the grain
of sand by the sea-shore. Yet He is no more
confined or limited to space than is thought to
the body. *In Him we live and move and have
our being* (Acts xvii. 28). *He fills the heavens
and the earth* (Jer. xxiii. 24). "Whither shall
I go from Thy spirit? If I ascend into heaven,
Thou art there ; if I descend into hell, Thou art
present ; if I take my wings early in the morning and dwell in the uttermost parts of the sea,

even there also Thy hand shall lead me and Thy right hand shall hold me" (Ps. cxxxviii.) "He is all in heaven, He is all on earth, He is not limited by any place, He is all in Himself in every place," says St. Augustine. If He could be absent from any place it would be possible for Him not to exist at all. But He is necessary. He could not have made Himself, nor could He have made any creature absolutely like Himself. He is immense, so that we cannot escape from Him ; eternal, so that all things are nothing before Him ; omniscient, so that we are laid open, without a secret, before Him.

Everything is penetrated by Him, yet His adorable purity remains untainted and His simplicity unmingled with that which it so intimately permeates. All we do, say, or think takes place in the being of the omnipresent God—a truth which, while it consoles on one hand, on the other gives a frightful character to acts of sin. We are in Him like fish in the sea. He is as intimately present in every being and in each atom as though that alone were the only point in existence. He legislates for one as for all, and concentrates all creation on it.

The Almighty is also immutable. There is no change in Him. Change implies ignorance, de-

cay, and imperfection. To change is to become
what one was not, or to cease being that which
one was. If one becomes that which he was
not, he was separated from it and did not exist
in this sense. If he loses what he was or had,
he ceases to exist in that point and is separated
from it. In either case he neither was nor is
absolute or perfect being. When he creates he
does not change ; the act and its conceptions
always existed immutably in the divine Mind.

As there never was a time when the Lord was
not in all the plenitude of His self-sufficient
majesty, He is always the self-same. *God is not
as man that He should lie, or the son of man
that He should change* (Num. xxiii. 13). *I
change not* (Mal. iii. 6). *He is without the
shadow of vicissitude* (James i. 17). "He
changes His works, but not His plans or counsels," said St. Augustine.

Then He is immutable. He is actually all
that He is. Unlike us—part in act and part in
potency—He is all act. To will and to do are
the same with Him. He is all His infinite possibility, actually present and living. HE IS A
SIMPLE ACT, as He is justly styled both by Aris-
totle and St. Thomas.

God is absolutely and infinitely simple, not
complex or in any way composed of parts. *God*

is spirit (John iv. 24). *The Lord is a spirit* (2 Cor. iii. 17). If composed He must have parts, material or spiritual; it makes no differ- ence which. If material, as in bodies, one part must be at one point and another at a different place, like hand and foot. He would not be en- tire in any of them, nor simple and absolute in any one of them, nor absolute at all.

If He be composed of spiritual or immaterial parts these parts would be distinct attributes, one of which would not be the other and none of them Himself totally. They would be limited in relation to each other and limited in relation to Himself. They would be circumscribed and limited attributes. He could only exist to the end of these limited attributes and not beyond them. He could not be infinite and absolute. The Necessary Being, therefore, cannot be com- posed in any manner. He is absolutely simple, and consequently all His attributes are identical with each other and with the divine essence.

Properly speaking, God has no perfections, which are our way of approaching to an hon- orable idea of him. The ineffable simplicity of the divine nature renders it impossible to form a just conception of ONE TRUE GOD. He is His own perfection, and that embraces all. Simplicity is the whole of God. It must be laid down as a fact, established by reason and religion, that there is perfect equality between all God's attributes—Himself, His being, and His adorable essence.

The holy doctors prove and inculcate this profound mystery very forcibly. St. Thomas thus expresses it: "In God being and essence are identical; the understanding of God is His essence; God's will is His essence; God is His own life; God is His own beatitude." St. Irenæus, in refuting the Gnostics, who impiously imputed human affections to God, thus expresses himself: "The Father of all is infinitely remote from human passions and feelings. He is simple and not compound; He is Himself all like to Himself; He is all equal because He is all spirit and intellect; He is like-membered, or all His members are the same." The expression is wonderful and unique —'Ομοιόχωλον. The same idea is found in Cicero, but the expression different (*Tusc.*, book i. chap. xxvii.)

God is absolutely simple, or one. *I am one* (Deut. xxxii. 39). He is unity itself; He only is oneness. The Infinite alone is absolutely one, because He is absolutely total. No creature is total or absolutely full and complete. There is no absolute concrete unity outside of God. Our thoughts, ideas, and souls in comparison with matter are simple, yet in themselves they are complex. All the faculties of the soul are distinct, and one is not the other. An atom is one in its centre only, which is not itself entirely. All created unity is a mere shadow of the incomprehensible unity of the ever-blessed God. He alone is one; He alone is simplicity itself.

Although there can be no real distinction between the divine perfections, nevertheless they are justly distinguished in our thoughts and conceptions. Justice and mercy offer different ideas to our minds. In God they are one and the same. This is caused by the fact that God presents Himself in a different manner or degree of esseity or light to His creatures. He puts Himself in a great variety of attitudes, acts, and relationship with us, as the sun in the heavens does not always present the same appearance to the world which he rules and enlightens. Morning, noon, and evening, and throughout the entire day, his aspects vary. We know that the self-subsisting essence of God is in each of the three Uncreated Persons of the Most Holy Trinity in its unity and simplicity, and we also know that the attributes are not synonyms. St. Bernard beautifully teaches the doctrine as follows: "Away with heretics who impiously assert that the greatness by which God is great, the goodness by which He is good, the wisdom by which He is wise, the justice by which He is just, and the divinity by which He is God, is not God!"

God is invisible. Although so intimately present in all His works, He was never seen by mortal, and thus gives room for faith, that we may win an eternal recompense by its exercise. *The King of ages, immortal and invisible, whom no man saw nor can see* (1 Tim. i. 17). It was an angel that conversed with Moses and gave the law, as the representative of the Most High. The Second Person was never seen until He became man and dwelt amongst us, the divine essence still remaining unseen.

He is incomprehensible, as defined by the Vatican Council. "The soul of Jesus Christ knows and sees God as plainly as He is seen and known" is a condemned proposition. He surpassed the combined understanding of all angels and saints. Not even the glory-strengthened eye of the Mother of God can see the plenitude of the divine nature. *Behold God is great beyond our knowledge* (Job xxxvi. 26). We are cautioned not to scrutinize His mysteries rashly.' *He who is a searcher of majesty shall be oppressed with glory* (Prov. xxv. 27).

The great First Cause is omnipotent; He can do all possible things, and His power is limited only by His perfections. He is the cause and the origin of all things besides Himself. All things else are contingent and imperfect, and could not have produced themselves. As there was a time when they were not, it follows as a necessary consequence that they were produced from nothing. But nothing short of infinite power could create a thing from nothing or preserve its existence when created. Therefore the Absolute Being is also omnipotent. This He assures by His own holy word: *O Lord, Lord, almighty King, there is none can resist Thy will* (Esther xiii. 9). *None can resist His will* (Isa. lv.) No words can express it. No ideas can conceive it properly. It costs Him no effort to call numberless possible worlds and creations out of nothing. Impossibility is no limit to Him. To such terrific power nothing is impossible, nothing is great or small. Our free-will alone seems to be a limit to Him, and we dare to brave His might.

He desires our salvation and that none should perish. By an abuse of His grace and their own free-will many resist Him. Even then He is not defeated, for He has provided an alternative. By primary and antecedent will He desires the salvation of all. It is but conditional and is based on our free acceptance of the conditions. If we reject His mercy there is the secondary will by which He decrees that obstinate sinners shall perish, for He is just.

Physical evils happen by His will, and they are good and necessary in the wise dispensations of His merciful providence. *Shall there be an evil in the city which the Lord hath not done?* (Amos iii. 6).

It is asked why God permits moral evils. Many heretics in former and recent times blasphemously assert that the all-holy God is the author of sin. Human lips could not utter a deeper impiety. The Holy Ghost declares *that the sinner and his wickedness are both hateful to God* (Wisdom). God *tempteth no man* (James i. 13). This is the will of God—your sanctification.

But He permits sin for wise and merciful purposes. The permission of evil implies grace. Without it neither angels nor men would be free ; and freedom is necessary for merit. A heaven of saints ready made was not God's plan, nor could it be a source of glory any more than other external manifestations of His wisdom and power. The fortitude

of the martyrs, the unbending perseverance of
the confessors, the nobility of human efforts,
and the heroism of the saints are based on
this grave permission, and all the varied glories
of the seats of bliss in Sion. It was this flooded the world with grace and caused the astounding mystery of the Redemption. Were
it not for this terrible truth little indeed would
be known of the wonders of divine mercy.
Power creates from nothing, but mercy brings
good from evil.

God is infinite wisdom; He knows us and all
things else, in their deepest and ultimate causes,
in Himself. All human and angelic knowledge
is but a ray of His light; all the various
tongues of men a broken accent of the Eternal
Word. He is the abyss of all possible worlds
and creations in all their order, harmony, and
variety of beings. *All things are naked and
open to His eyes* (Heb. iv. 13), even our most
secret actions and thoughts. How terrible,
then, the agony of the lost one, to feel that he
lies open and transparent before the gaze of
God's infallible wisdom!

"God's foreknowledge has as many witnesses
as there are prophets," says Tertullian. His
all-seeing eye takes in at a single glance all
things, past, present, and future—all possible

6

things, all even that never will occur, but would occur if certain conditions were actuated. Had Tyre and Sidon but beheld the miracles done in Corozain and Bethsaida they would not have perished.

"Nothing," says St. Augustine, "is future to God. He fills all time, and His knowledge embraces all things; they are not future but present, and should be called knowledge and not foreknowledge." His knowledge does not destroy our freedom, determine our acts, nor impair our liberty. These are foreseen because they occur; they do not occur because they are foreseen. We are free as air, and we know this by experience. God's word confirms our innate conviction: *Thou hast made all things in wisdom* (Ps. ciii. 24). It is not in the extreme of possible excellence that this wisdom manifests itself, but in the harmony of creation, in the adaptation of means to their end, like light and the eye. It is possible for God to create differently and more perfectly, but His wisdom would then be no more conspicuous.

The moral attributes of God are distinguished from the metaphysical and have a relation to the duties and obligations of man. They are the plenitude of all virtues in God and in their infinite extent. They are justice, patience, mercy, etc., etc.

God is truth. He is all truth, in all its departments—essential and absolute truth. *God is true* (Rom. iii. 4). He does not lie (John iii. 33) ; it is impossible (Tit. i. 2). Everything is what it is in His sight, and no more. All truth in science and in creation is a derivation of the truth of God. Whatever is true in them is so because it is in accord with Him, and whatever is not conformable to Him is a distortion and a lie. It is difficult to conceive any greater disorder than a falsehood in religion, a lie about God. It is excessive misery and vice, and its wilful abettors are no less odious than were the priests of the idols.

Justice is resplendent among the moral perfections of our most compassionate Creator. *Thou art just, O Lord, and thy judgment is right* (Ps. cxviii. 137). It is infallibly certain that *He will render to every man according to his works* (Matt. xvi. 27). True, in this world the wicked often prosper and the just suffer. But human life is only the beginning of our existence, and the earth is not the theatre of God's infinite justice. It is too narrow, mortal man is too weak, and all time too short. It is for eternity that the immortal spirit will suffer or be recompensed. Full justice in this corner of creation would be not only impossible, but would not be in harmony with our condition or advantages, and our destiny, and the laws of our redemption. Sufferings are the special marks of God's favor and invariably the portion of the righteous. The woes of the Man-God are among the most frightful mysteries of the Gospel. *Woe to you rich, woe to you who now laugh and rejoice! Blessed are the poor, the meek, the merciful.*

Lest we may be tempted to doubt God's justice, He frequently displays portions of it on earth. He bestows natural rewards on natural virtues; no sin will ever pass unpunished and no virtue unrewarded. "Good and wicked princes have sat on the same throne, to show," says St. Augustine, "that the favors of fortune are no test of righteousness." Divine justice is so perfect that its punishments are even magnificent, yet most dreadful because of their truthful justice. In the hopeless home of the lost there is not even the shadow of a pain beyond the strict demands of austere justice.

The entire world is a necropolis because of one sin. The faultless rigor and stern demands of justice are only satisfied fully by the cruci-

fixion and death of the just Judge Himself.
Who knows the omnipotence of divine wrath,
the penalty of rejected mercy and despised
love? It is a divine necessity; every jail and
gibbet on earth confirms the solemn truth. If
there be no future penalties, neither can there
be future rewards, and all man's existence
must end in the dust and dishonor of the
tomb.

God is infinitely holy because He is essential purity—holy in Himself and the principle
of all holiness among angels and men. His
holiness cannot grow nor increase, as among
men, for it is His essence. In Him it is substantial, for it is Himself; it is also a quality,
like all His moral attributes, for He is also
holy. All our holiness consists in the love of
God; all God's holiness consists in the love of
Himself. How infinite His purity! The sera-
phim cry out incessantly, *Holy, holy, holy, Lord
God of Hosts* (Isa. vi. 3). His holiness is so
absolute that if, for the committal of but one
sin, all men would be converted, He could not
sanction it any more than He could cease to be
God—no, not even if earth, purgatory, and hell
with their countless hosts would by that act be
turned into paradise. It was a sin that nailed
Christ to the cross; sin is man's only evil.

We are to be holy because our heavenly Father is holy, and perfect because He is perfect. Our moral attributes are in fearful dissimilarity with the holiness and perfection of the thrice holy God. Yet He is our model, and we must copy Him in the tenor of our lives and actions if we would reign with Him for ever. To fear God and keep His commandments is all man's worth.

ᴵ God is love. He throws all His divine perfections into one—love. It is a love infinite, eternal, immutable, omnipotent, and so throughout heaven and earth, the three dispensations, creation, redemption, the Church, all that is, are produced by love. The chastisements of the future life are the penalty of its rejection. It is a frightful disorder when the creature rejects the proffered love and friendship of his Maker and tramples under foot His just commandments, having their foundation on the divine and human natures and the just relation between both. ᴵ

You must pardon from your very heart your greatest enemy, or your transgressions will never be forgiven you by the most compassionate Father, who will go on rewarding for all eternity for even a cup of cold water given for His sake to your needy brother. If this brother be your

enemy the greater still will be the reward. Love,
like simplicity, is the whole of God.

Conspicuous among the moral attributes is
mercy. It is infinite; it is a multitude of tender compassions and is another side of love,
for it pardons after repeated injuries, and craves
to be asked. What causes the loss of the soul
but the rejection of proffered mercy? The Almighty seems to be indebted to us for this gorgeous attribute, which, when copied, almost dei-
fies the creature. *Be you merciful, as your
heavenly Father is merciful.* He has no sorrows Himself to relieve, no wants to supply.
There is mercy everywhere—earth is flooded
with it, heaven gleams with it, purgatory is its
special creation. 'Even the regions of perpetual
night, where neither hope nor rest ever comes,
are less dark because of some excesses of its
lights, like a sunbeam in the cell of the condemned to whom human sympathy is denied.
Anything reasonable may be asked of Mercy.
It brought down the Son of God from heaven
and adorned creation with the splendors of our
redemption. Mercy is one of God's perfections.
Love is the harmony of them all. Benignity,
goodness, and all the moral attributes are established by the light of reason and taught in
Holy Writ: *He is benignant and merciful, pa-*

tient and of much mercy (Joel ii. 13); *He is infinite beatitude in Himself* (1 Tim. vi. 15). He is infinite beauty, power, glory, majesty, riches—an immense ocean of being, possessing in their plenitude and in every degree all real and possible goods in the unity of the most transcending simplicity.

The Almighty is free; His external acts are all free. He was not compelled by any necessity to create; an eternity, in fact, had passed before anything was made; yet His essential glory and bliss were nothing less when He dwelt in the uncreated solitude of His adorable trinity in unity. He could have made all things in a different manner; the whole magnificent machinery of a thousand worlds could be altered; the immensity of space could be filled with millions of orbs and peopled with intelligent beings or not, according to His free and intelligent will: *He hath done all things whatsoever He would* (Ps. cxiii. 3).

His spotless liberty is absolutely holy, wise, and perfect. It is limited by the perfection only of His nature, nor can it suffer the taint of sin or error. His decrees and the covenants which the divine condescension made with His creatures proceed from His holy will and are in harmony with the plan and purpose of creation and with the salvation of the human family. Our liberty consists in choosing, and in our fallen state the perilous choice runs between good and evil. The latter is too frequently preferred, and the preference is licentious and slavish, for no man is free who is not free from himself. If he is the slave of base passions and of Satan, if he is the tool of his own spite and malice and the victim of self-love, with what ·freedom is he free? *The truth alone can make you free.* God being truth essential, He is infinitely free and His liberty unlimited.

Our merciful Creator is the beginning and the end of all things. We came from Him, and, by the necessity of our nature, unto Him must we return. As rivers rush to the ocean, so do we hasten on to return to our origin and source. Heaven is union with God, hell separation from God. God's being is the creature's home; God's end is Himself and ours also; His beatitude is ours, His interests ours; we have one common cause, and the sins committed against Him are universal evils. We suffer for the transgressions of others and share in their graces. One saint would be missed from heaven, and his vacant throne would be an unseemly gap in the ranks of bliss. We are members of Christ's mystic body and members of each other. Every

7

lost soul is an increase of torments to the hopeless prisoners in their eternal dungeon.

Liberty, will, power, love, goodness, and all moral attributes pertain to God, and the denial of any one of them is at least material atheism, for in the absence of any of them God would not be perfect. ' Man, indeed, would be superior to God, for man possesses these attributes in a measure or degree. Reason proves that the Almighty is endowed with all these perfections to an unlimited extent, for in man there exist ideas, vestiges, and degrees of these excellences.

We have aspirations which nothing short of the Infinite can satisfy ; we have longings perpetually checked by a sense of feebleness—longings which are circumscribed within the limits of a narrow prison. An admirable adaptation exists between the nature of God and the nature of man. God possesses in its plenitude all that we need ; He is sufficient for Himself and for all His creatures, and the superabundance of His riches supplies our deficiency. We sigh for good—He is all goodness ; we pine for strength—He is omnipotent ; we thirst for truth—He is truth essential ; we languish for life—He is life itself ; we seek peace—He is everlasting rest, and joy, and happiness. The creature thirsts for the influx of the Creator, and the more excellent the creature's nature the greater are his wants. It is asserted that these aspirations, unrealized within us, seek abroad for their adequate and co-extensive objects, and, suppressing their limits, run out into an infinitude and thus create a God. This theory of unbelievers furnishes an undeniable, self-evident proof of the existence of the merciful God and of His divine perfections, based on the very nature of the soul. It is within us and none can rob us of it : *No thief can break through and steal.*

I AM, THEREFORE GOD IS. My existence establishes the truth of His. This is more than demonstration—it is intuition, flashing on the mind with the conviction of a self-evident axiom. It is God's handwriting, indelibly imprinting His holy name upon every human heart, whether in the enlightened circles of society, in the desert, or in the islands of the sea. I am weak, inconstant, imperfect, dependent. A thousand worlds could flow into my soul and still leave it a barren waste.

Then there exists a Being immutable, eternal, omnipotent, infinitely great and good. For it is preposterous to suppose that the imperfect, the almost nothing, could exist, and the perfect, the real and substantial, should not exist ; that man can be and God cannot be!

Pining, weary, and languishing, the soul thirsts for the true and the real, for something better than all it beholds. Wealth, honor, fame, power, learning—they were all weighed and found wanting; they left the soul dispirited and disappointed. Then there exists a Being greater than all greatness, infinitely great, and good, and beautiful, and true. It is a cruel mockery to assert that the noble aspirations of the soul tend to nothing real; that they are mere illusions thrown out from the heart, like the phantoms that beguile the traveller at night and lure him to his doom. Then the insatiable thirst of the soul for the true, the good, and the real is but a deceit. Then there are attractions without an object, effects without a cause, and creatures without a creator. O abyss of misery into which infidelity mercilessly· hurls its victims after robbing them of rest, and peace, and of themselves! Oh! no; conscience, prayer, sorrow, suffering, and even death, convince us that we are irresistibly hastening on to the Infinite, to our Father and our God.

I am, therefore God is. I am an intelligence, or love, an energy; then God is all these, and more besides, in an infinite manner. I affirm of Him, without any limits, all the perfections I possess. How could there be a perfection in

me, if it were not in God? I am, therefore
God is. If I destroy the limits of these
my perfections, and add infinite to each, they
all inevitably reach the Author of my being.
He, then, is infinitely perfect and possesses in
infinite manner all I so sadly need. Parched
with thirst, pining from want, and consumed
by longings, I turn to my merciful Creator
and discover that He possesses in their plenitude all I need and my spirit yearns for.
May He not grant it when I suffer so bitterly
for the privation? He is too high; I cannot
reach Him; may He not find a way to reach
me?

Communication is the natural bent and tendency of all excellence and perfection. Learning loves to display itself, beauty to be seen,
and goodness will bestow with a generous hand.
How much more is not this the case with infinite love, infinite goodness, bounty, and compassion, especially when the gift does not exhaust nor impoverish the giver, but, on the
contrary, enriches him! To give is God's nature; His desire and His glory are to bestow.
He outstrips Himself and overfloods all creation with a deluge of His favors.

The sun does not bestow his light more free-
ly, nor the fountain its waters, than God be-

stows good things on all His creatures. *He maketh His sun to shine on the good and the bad, and raineth on the just and the unjust* (Matt. v. 45). He bestows His vast creation and all its splendors, heaven and all its riches, on each of the just, and superadds all that Omnipotence will ever achieve. He is Himself our reward exceeding great, and nothing less than the Infinite can satisfy the God-like spirit. Nothing is too good, if we only accept. Worlds He deems too insignificant for His children; not merely these does He lavish on us, but all the plenitude of His ineffable being and all His infinite perfections. See Him in the manger; see Him on the cross; see Him in the Holy Eucharist. The whole of God is the property of the most humble communicant at His holy table.

There is for each a throne of glory prepared that outshines the splendors of the starry heavens, and a kingdom compared with which all the wealth of the universe is but poverty. The *eye hath not seen, nor ear heard, neither hath it entered into the heart of man to conceive what God hath prepared for them that love Him* (1 Cor. ii. 9). All that He has and is becomes our own on the condition that we love Him and keep His commandments. In this is all man's dignity, and not in the vain pomp and pageantry of the earth nor in its godless splendors.

In our belief, and in the tenor of our lives and actions, we must honor all the divine perfections, and all of them at once, or rather Himself as universal perfection.

Amid trials and sufferings God's adorable attributes are our consolation and our support. We can rest on them in security and peace, like the child in the bosom of the most tender parent, and prepare ourselves to join, after a short time, the myriad hosts in the universal hymn: *To Him that sitteth on the throne, and to the Lamb, benediction and praise and glory and power and honor for ever and ever. Amen* (Apoc. v. 13).

CONFERENCE III. .

ON THE DIVINITY OF OUR LORD JESUS CHRIST, THE SECOND PERSON OF THE BLESSED TRINITY.

Doctrine explained—Meaning of Terms—Essence—Generation—Procession—Nature—Person—Dogma taught by the Church—Ten Proofs abridged—Jesus Christ true God and true Man—Common Sense scarce—Silly Philosophers—Mythology—The Desired of all Nations—Greater than Abraham—Typical Characters—David and the Prophets—The Messias born in a Stable—The Star of Jacob and of Araby the Blest—Rachel and Bethlehem—Herod and the unclean Spirits—Egypt and Nazareth—Comparisons—The Widow of Sarepta and the Widow of Naim—A Dilemma for Infidels—Sinai—Thabor and Golgotha—Conversion of a Malefactor, an Infidel, and a Mob—Abraham's Faith renewed—Death, Resurrection, and Ascension—Jonas and Elias—Ye Men of Galilee—All bear Testimony—Immortality on Earth—Moral Reflections—Emmanuel—Jehovah—Names of Essence belong to our Lord.

I.

From the womb before the day-star I begot thee (Ps. cix.)

MY BRETHREN:

There is but ONE TRUE GOD, the Creator and sovereign Lord of heaven and earth, and of all things. He exists in three divine persons, the

Father and the Son and the Holy Ghost, who are all one, having one and the same divine nature; and they are perfectly equal to each other in all things. The adorable mystery of the Blessed Trinity will be fully explained when I shall first have treated of the divinity of our Lord Jesus Christ, the second Person, who became man and died for our salvation. The divinity of our Lord being once established, the august mystery of the Trinity is virtually proved.

For the better understanding of the subject permit me to explain the meaning of some terms. Essence means that which strictly constitutes anything; it differs from nature, which has a wider range. The essence of man, for instance, consists in his having a rational soul united with a body. The divine essence consists in the necessity of God's existence, which includes all perfections. Being is God's proper name, which is called in Greek "To' "Ον"; in Latin, "Ens"; and Hebrew, "Jehovah." It is equivalent to "I am" in English.

In God nature, essence, substance, existence are all one because of His infinite simplicity. Person is an intelligent, free principle of action, as man. Human personality differs from the divine in this respect: that the human personality implies the negation of union with any other subject by way of dependence but in God. Person is not distinct from the divine essence, for each has the same divine nature and the plenitude of the undivided Godhead; the personality alone is proper.

Generation is an act by which a living being from its own substance produces another living being, and like unto itself, by virtue of this act. Procession in the Blessed Trinity implies the origin of one divine Person from another, or from two, as one principle, as the procession of the Holy Ghost from the Father and the Son. The Son is begotten or born of the Father. In the Blessed Trinity each Person imparts totally all that He is to another, and retains but His personality, which is also imparted virtually but not constitutively. The Father is always the Father, the Son is always the Son, and the Holy Ghost always the Holy Ghost. This is God's manner of being, and is so necessary that if it were different He would not exist at all nor anything else. The Son is the second divine Person. His equivalent name is the WORD—VERBUM in Latin, LOGOS in Greek—which means that He is the total, permanent, and substantial expression of the Father, like Him in everything and one with Him. The names of Jesus Christ,

Messias, Saviour, Redeemer, and others, appertain to Him because of the work of our redemption which He accomplished.

He differs in this respect from the other adorable Persons, that He alone became man for our sake. He was born of the Blessed Virgin Mary and has two natures, the divine and human, in one person; He is true God and true man, as in each of us there are two natures, spirit and matter, united so intimately as to form but one person—man.

The human nature of our Lord being now conceded, I will present to your consideration the divine, and for your edification adduce a few of the many reasons why the holy Catholic Church, which He founded, believes and teaches that Jesus Christ is God and consubstantial with the Father.

The Arians, the Socinians, and other unbelievers, while conceding Christ's superexcellence over all creatures, denied His divinity. The Word, or Son, has two generations—one in time, when He was born of the Virgin Mary, and the other eternal and incessant by the necessity of the divine nature. The Psalmist introduces the Son as saying: *The Lord hath said to me, Thou art my Son, this day have I begotten thee* (ii. 7). Again: *The Lord said to my Lord,*

. . . . *From the womb before the day-star I begot Thee* (Ps. cix.) His generation *is from the days of eternity*, said Micheas (v. 2). The eternal generation of the Son is, then, plainly taught in Holy Writ. St. John inculcates it in the most clear manner possible: *In the beginning was the Word, and the Word was with God, and the Word was God. All things were made by Him, and without Him was nothing made that was made* (John i.) When all things were made by Him, in common with the Father and the Holy Ghost, He never was made, but He exists with and is born of the Father from eternity. He is therefore true God, God Himself, perfectly equal to the Father. "He is Light of Light, God of God, consubstantial with the Father," says the Church (Nicene Creed).

Jesus Christ is the true God of mankind. Outside of Him is sin, and sorrow, and ignorance; in Him is light, and peace, and rest. Blessed is he who can say with the Church, I believe in Jesus Christ, the Son of God, equal to the Father from eternity in power, and wisdom, and in all things. Christ possesses the treasures of the Deity. *He is the true light, that enlightens every man that cometh into the world.* It is through Him only that he can come to the Father. *He is the way, the truth, and the life.* Thrice happy those who possess this faith, which imparts real and eternal life.

The divinity of our Lord is the foundation on which society, law, and order rest. Its denial would bury the world in darkness, misery, and vice; its denial, in fact, will be the harbinger of the reign of Antichrist, when time itself will cease to run.

Unbelievers deny the divine nature of the Son, thus impugning the essence of God, the fecundity of the divine nature, and effacing from the Supreme Being the idea of infinite perfection. That the Infinite should condescend to assume our nature, suffer, and die is, indeed, a mystery beyond the reach of our understanding. Without the light of a divine revelation and the declaration of the prophets, who foretold the marvellous event, the people of God had not known it and the world had not been prepared to receive so divine a truth. The malice of man's transgression could be adequately repaired by no less a being than God. If the mediator of our peace were merely a man the mediator himself would need another mediator to render his atonement acceptable. It was necessary, then, in the divine counsels that our mediator should be God and man both. The character, then, given of the Messias is not only human but is absolutely divine. The sanctity of our Lord's maxims and teachings, the wisdom of His laws, and His integrity of life are lauded to the skies by modern free-thinkers. Solon or Lycurgus, Socrates or Plato, cannot be compared with Him; they concede to Him every excellence short of divinity—that He was the greatest benefactor of the human race, the brightest light ever shed on this world.

Consistency is as rare as common sense. This concession illustrates how every spirit that raises itself up against the wisdom and power of God, from Satan down, stultifies itself. Now, if Christ is not God there never arose a greater enemy of our race, and He has firmly planted on earth the empire of Satan. For in this impious supposition the splendors of His mission served but to bury the world in idolatry and vice, and incurably corrupt the heart of man. The ever-blessed God Himself would indeed in that case be the author of this universal desolation.

We know, according to the infallible teachings of the Church, that Jesus Christ is God and the beginning and the end of all things. One of the first proofs of His divinity is that He was promised to the human race from the beginning of the world. Adam was consoled with a promise that his transgression would be repaired, and he beheld from afar the Redeemer whom his disobedience made necessary to his race. It was to prepare for His coming that empires rose and fell for four thousand years. He was the main object of all important events. Babylon and Macedon and Rome, Cyrus and Cæsar, the Pentateuch and the *Iliad*, all the arts .and sciences, and the tide of time itself, wore their face to the dawn and rising of the Star of Hope that consoled Job in all his afflictions. He was foretold by all the prophets, typified by all the figures, foreshadowed by all the sacrifices of the Old Law. Jesus was the end of all things.

From among all the nations of the earth God selects a particular people to be the depository of this great promise. He makes them the sacerdotal caste of the human race; He places in their hands the badges of their authority, and besides leaves the world to learn from them all correct information regarding this wide-spread hope which first fell on the human heart and reminded the sad exile of his lost paradise. On the dispersion of the human race from the plains of Sennaar each family took with them some seedlings of this precious plant and bequeathed them to their descendants as a sacred trust. But they were soon disfigured, degenerating into fond fables, and were subverted to the worst passions. Yet there is no mythology so dark that it does not contain the promise of some forfeited golden age; and one pagan fable records that of all the treasures which man received at his birth from Heaven hope alone was left when he had lost all besides. Darkness and the shadow of death brooded over the face of the globe until it became a wide Haceldama of violence and crime that called for another deluge or a restorer. All things, says the apostle, *groaned and labored to bring forth the Promise.* The saints implored *the heavens to open and the clouds to rain down the just one* (Isaias xlv.)

Cyrus and the Baptist were honored each by a particular prediction, but only in reference to Him who was to come, and that the fulfilment of proximate events should confirm the truth of all that was foretold of the Messias. He was promised from the beginning; typified by an entire people; expected by all ages; all the just, like Henoch, walked in the brightness of this faith; parents taught their children to lisp it until it became the belief of the whole world, propagated from age to age, and the very oracles of the Gentiles, whether at Memnon or at the fountains of Egeria, muttered the marvellous event.

He was hailed, not for an isolated purpose, but as the salvation of the human race, the legislator of all ages, the light of all nations, the one who would destroy and take away the sins of the world, fill the earth with the Spirit of God, and bring down everlasting peace. What a magnificent preparation!

Prophecy is the foretelling of some future event which could be known to God only. It is an infallible criterion of truth. Every event, every personage, every verse in the Old Testament are all prophetic or typical, and must be fulfilled in the New. *The heavens and the earth shall pass away, but not an iota shall pass away until all is fulfilled.* I present a few of these prophecies; each is conclusive evidence of the truth.

A Child is born to us, and a Son is given to us, and the government is upon his shoulders; and His name shall be called Wonderful, Counsellor, God, the Mighty, the Father of the world to come, the Prince of Peace (Isaias ix. 6). *Behold, a virgin shall conceive, and bear a Son, and His name shall be called Emmanuel* (that is, God with us) (Isaias vii. 14). Micheas says: Out of thee, O Bethlehem, *shall He come forth*

8

unto me that is to be the ruler in Israel, and His going forth is from the beginning, from the days of eternity (ch. v.) Here is plainly foretold the birth of a wonderful Child, the son of a spotless Virgin, born in Bethlehem and declared to have an existence from eternity. The Child Jesus is God; for none but God is eternal. To sound reason it will always be clear that these and other predictions are too well authenticated to be doubted, too explicit to be misunderstood, and too palpably verified in the person of Christ not to be assented to.

All the renowned men of former times, the saints under both the patriarchal and levitical law whose greatness amazed mankind, were but types, but prophetic characters, individually and collectively, but images of Christ, and each foreshadowed but one feature of His life and ministry—Abel, His death; Melchisedech, His priesthood; Job, His afflictions; Abraham, His paternity; Moses and Aaron, His ministry; Solomon, His wisdom. Great must He be when a bare shadow of but one of His prerogatives made the man who bore it, like the prophet's mantle, the wonder of all ages. If not God, our Lord could not claim to be greater than His figurative representatives.

Was He greater than Abraham—that chief so

renowned that the Hebrew nation believed themselves superior to all other people because they
were the children of Abraham; that patriarch
so illustrious that, with all His magnificent titles,
Jehovah took the additional title of the God of
Abraham to show that the homage of a man
so holy was as honorable to His Sovereignty as
the title of the God of armies and of empires?
Was He more wonderful than Moses—that man
powerful in word and work, the mediator of a
new alliance; the good of Pharao, who broke the
yoke of Egypt, saved His people, fed them from
heaven; nature's lord, who spoke to God on the
holy mountain and appeared before all Israel
brilliant with glory? Now, if He was not the
everlasting God He did equal His types, and the
Jews may have asked without impiety, *Art thou
greater than our father Abraham and the prophets who are dead?* He was the reality of
every fleeting shadow, and the combined greatness of all centred in Him like streams in the
ocean.

Collecting all these miraculous characters,
types, figures, sacrifices, histories, forming the
prophetic movement of the world during four
thousand years, the preparation is so magnificent that if Christ, its object, were but a great
man merely, God Himself, who had ushered Him

in with so much glory, is Himself the author of
the error of all who have adored Christ for nineteen centuries as God.   Far be it from any human heart to make the All-Holy the author of
sin!   Jesus Christ is true God ; the Father and
He are one ; He is the Second Person of the
adorable Trinity.

The prophecies are fulfilled.   The Messias is
born on earth, at the hour of midnight, and in a
stable, as had been spoken by the prophets inspired by God.   The cradle of Him who sur-
rounded His tomb with glory and with the wonders of His magnificence witnesses the most stupendous miracles.   Angels fill the midnight air
with hymns of joy, announcing glory to God
and peace to man.   A star of great brilliancy ap
pears in the East and rests over Judea.   The
three Chaldean sages, recognizing this as the
star foretold by the prophet, faithful to its voice
and still more to the instructions of divine grace
which moved their hearts, have set out from
their country and now cast their diadems at the
feet of Him whom they adore as God, despite
His humiliations and poverty.   A cruel and jealous king, apprehensive for his own life and for
his kingdom, attempts to destroy the new-born
Child.   Protected by Omnipotence from all the
malicious plots, the Child escapes the massacre

of the male children of Bethlehem and the vicinity, and passes His first years in Egypt. By a fresh command He returns to His native land and remains subject and obedient to His parents until His thirtieth year.

Reaching the age of maturity, He stands before the world, begins His public mission, proclaims His kingdom, preaches His doctrine, establishes the Church, institutes the sacraments, and confirms all by His miracles, and proves to all ages, present and future, that He is God, the Creator of all things and the Redeemer of the world. The prophecies which foretold Him, the miracles which preceded and accompanied His birth, the prodigies which He wrought, and all the miracles attendant on His sufferings and death on the cross prove the fact still more forcibly. The sublimity of His doctrines and of His moral code, the manner in which He establishes them and in which He confirms them, the sanctity of His life, His promises, the establishment and preservation of His Church, are each and all palpable evidences of the fact that Jesus Christ is the God who made us, our Sovereign Lord and Master, and the Judge of the living and the dead.

John the Baptist, the greatest of all men, declared himself unworthy to perform even the

most menial offices for Him. No sooner, in fact,
is Jesus Christ baptized in the Jordan than the
heavens are opened, and the Holy Ghost descends upon Him in the form of a dove, while
the voice of the Eternal Father declares Him to
be His Son. The unclean spirits owned His
power, and by the mouths of the possessed declare Him to be God.

I present in an abridged form ten of the principal arguments by which is proved unanswer-
ably our Lord's divinity :

First. It is proved by the many places in
Scripture where our blessed Lord is absolutely
called God : *And His name shall be called Em-*
manuel (Isaias vii. 14). St. Matthew applies this
to Christ (i. 23): *Which means, God with us.*
In the same place (Isaias ix. 6) it is added: *His*
name shall be called Wonderful, Counsellor,
God, the Mighty, the Father of the world to
come, and the Prince of Peace. *The name they*
shall call Him, the Lord our just one (Jehovah)
(Jer. xxiii. 6). *The Word was made flesh and*
dwelt amongst us (John i. 14). *My Lord and*
my God, said St. Thomas (John xx. 28). *He is*
true God and life eternal (1 John v. 20).
God blessed for ever (Rom. ix. 5). *The great*
God and our Saviour Jesus Christ (Titus ii. 13).
He is called by the name of essence, Elohim—

Jehovah—(Isaias **xxxv.**) Here and in the following instances I must limit my quotations in the interests of conciseness ; one text is abundant.

Secondly. Our Lord's divinity is proved from the conviction of the Jews that He asserted it, and which He confirmed. If misunderstood He would have made the correction, as He always did ; how much more necessary to do so in this instance! For this assertion of His divinity was the ostensible cause of His death. He promises to bestow eternal life, the same as the Father, and adds : *I and the Father are one* (John **x.**) His opponents attempted to stone Him for blasphemy, and common honesty would have required Him to disavow His words if He were not God. It is clear that He was not understood in that broad sense in which prophets and good men are called gods and the sons of God. The Jews sought to kill Him because He said that God was His Father, making Himself equal to God (*ibid.*) Whatever the Father does He does. *As the Father raiseth up the dead and giveth life, so the Son also. Neither doth the Father judge any man, but hath given all judgment to the Son* (John **v.** 19-21). It was on this charge that He was made prisoner and was tried in public court by the high-priest, who adjured Him *by the name of the living God that thou tell us if thou be the Christ, the Son of God* (Matt. xxvi. 63). Our Lord not only answers affirmatively, but He claims the highest prerogative of supreme dominion. He will come *in the clouds of heaven* to judge the living and the dead. *The high-priest rent his garments, saying, He hath blasphemed;* and they all judged Him worthy of death. They forced Pilate to execute the sentence.

Thirdly. It is proved by the testimony of the Father on the Jordan: *This is my beloved Son* (Matt. iii. 17), on Thabor (Luke ix. 35), before the Gentiles (John xii. 38).

Fourthly. By the texts attributing the divine nature to our Lord: *In the name of Jesus every knee shall bow, and every tongue should confess that the Lord Jesus Christ is in the glory of God the Father* (Phil. ii. 10, 11). *The fulness of the Divinity dwells bodily in Him* (Col. i. 23).

Fifthly. The many testimonies that attribute all the divine works and perfections to our Lord prove Him to be God. He claims as His own all that the Father has, and that they hold all things in common (John xvi. 15). This in a creature would be an impious usurpation. The creation of all things from nothing and their pre-

servation are His works (John i.; Heb. i. 3, 10).
Eternity, immortality, immutability appertain to
Him. These words of the Psalmist are applied
by St. Paul to Christ: *Thou shalt change them,
and they shall be changed; but Thou art the
self-same, and Thy years shall not fail* (Heb.
i. 12). *Jesus Christ yesterday, and to-day; and
the same for ever* (ib. xiii. 8). He is omniscient;
He knows man's heart and thoughts : *Thou
knowest all things* (John xxi. 17). He is omnipotent, *Alpha and Omega, the beginning and
the end, who is and who was and who is to come*
(Apoc. i. 8). He in many places claims omni-
presence, and declares that He has His mansion
equally with the Father in the souls of the just
(Matt. xviii. 20). He will be with His ministers
wherever they are, *and all days even to the consummation of the world* (Matt. xxviii. 20).

. II.

Sixthly. St. Peter and the disciples confessed
Jesus Christ to be, not the adopted, but the true
and natural Son of God: *Thou art Christ, the
Son of the living God* (Matt. xvi. 16). Jesus is
Christ, the Son of God (1 John i. 3). *I believe
that Jesus Christ is the Son of God* (Acts viii.
37). None can be saved who does not believe
that Christ is God (John iii. 18). He who be-

9

lieveth in Him hath life everlasting; but he who is incredulous *shall not see life, but the wrath of God abideth on him* (ib. iii. 36). Our Lord demanded faith in Himself from the man who was born blind: *Dost thou believe in the Son of God? I believe, Lord; and falling down he adored Him* (ib. ix. 35, 38).

Seventhly. His adoration as God is often demanded, *that all may honor the Son as they honor the Father* (John v. 23). *Every knee shall bend before Him* (Phil. xi. 10). *All the angels of God shall adore Him* (Heb. i. 6). All creatures shall worship Him in the same manner as the Father: *To Him who sitteth on the throne, and to the Lamb, be benediction and honor and glory and power for ever and ever* (Apoc. v. 13).

Eighthly. Our Lord's divinity is still further established by the many miracles which He performed in His own name and by His own power. He frequently attributed these miracles to the Father as well as to Himself, in order to inculcate the unity of natures and the distinction of persons. These miracles were wrought to confirm His doctrines, especially His divinity. He conferred the same power on the apostles, to be used at their discretion.

Ninthly. Our blessed Lord's divine nature is,

moreover, vindicated by the titles which He claims for Himself : *I am the way, and the truth, and the life* (John xiv. 6). *I am the light of the world* (ib. viii. 12). *I am the resurrection and the life* (ib. xi. 25).

Tenthly. The Redeemer promises eternal life by His own right and title : *I give them life everlasting* (John x. 28). *I will raise him up in the last day* (John vi. 55). Here it is proved that He is the Lord of death and life. The apostle declares that in Him only is salvation. *There is no other name under heaven whereby we must be saved* (Acts iv. 12).

In several places He is called the *Son, the Begotten, the Only-Begotten Son of God,* which cannot be understood of an adopted son or of a simply just and good man, but only of the eternal and substantial Son of God, the Second Person of the blessed Trinity. In one or two instances He insinuates the superiority of the Father ; but this has reference to His human nature only, surely inferior to the divine and uncreated. *Show us the Father, and it sufficeth us,* said St. Philip. *O Philip! said Jesus, how long am I with you, and you know me not ? He who seeth me seeth my Father. . . . The Father and I are one.*

We are connected with Adam by an uninterrupted chain of prophets, and not a link will be missing until the second coming·of the Messias. The first are our fathers in the faith ; many of them seemed the very depositaries of omnipotent power. Samson before the gates of Gaza, Josue at the fords of the Jordan, and Moses at the Red Sea appeared to wield uncreated might. But upon a close inspection, in their very strength even was exhibited their dependence, despite the external *éclat* of the work. Jesus Christ never displayed the imperfection of dependence, necessary in the creature but not necessary in Him as God. All His miraculous works were exempt from this feature ; and it was here that the least of His works was greater and more perfect than the mightiest works of those renowned men.

By his rod Moses wrought all his miracles ; without it he was as weak as any man in the tents of Israel. Our Lord performed the most stupendous miracles without speaking a word ; the touch of the hem of His garment cured the most inveterate diseases. True, Elias raised the dead to life; yet see the struggle, the death-agony of his emaciated frame as he crouches over the remains of the dead boy. He holds not the key of life and death. But the Son of Mary raised the dead to life as easily as He performed the most ordinary actions. *All things live to Him.* The dead listen to Him *and hear His voice* as attentively as the living. The slumber of an infant is not more readily broken than was the cold sleep of the ruler's daughter and of the son of the widow of Naim. At the first sound of the voice of Jesus the myriad dead will start to life as readily as creation had risen from nothing at his *fiat*. Such is the omnipotence of our Lord; His works wear no mark of dependence.

History paints her sibyls and pythonesses as frenzied while uttering their guessing oracles. Even the prophets of God, when reading the future, were seized with a holy enthusiasm, but without detriment to reason or propriety. In some instances prophecy awoke at the sound of the lyre. Evidently the secrets of the future were not drawn from the depths of their own soul.

Our Lord prophesied as He spoke. The mysteries hidden in the womb of time were not sudden lights poured on His mind, nor did they thrill by their startling revelations. To His all-seeing eye they were the most familiar objects. The city of David trodden to the dust, her priests and maidens sold into slavery, the last day, the sentence of doom, and the fiery abyss—nothing could disturb the tranquillity of His mind but the sight of sin, as manifested at the grave of Lazarus, an image of a soul dead to the grace of God.

Whenever the inspired writers mentioned the omnipotent Ruler of heaven and earth, oppressed with the magnificence of the subject, after exhausting the power of language they would seize upon imagery in order to convey their conceptions. They justly represent God *as poising the world on three fingers, holding the seas in His hand, walking on the winds, and grasping the lightning.* When our Lord speaks to His Father He uses only the plain and familiar language of a son. His language is, *holy Father, just Father.* He speaks on equal terms, and He uses calm and familiar expressions, as one accustomed to the crown and sceptre of his Father.

Although Moses did not transmit the miraculous power to his descendants, and although he did not possess the divine power of remitting sins, claiming no higher distinction than of being the humble servant of God, he yet took every precaution that after death his remains should not be an occasion of idolatry to his people. He died alone and was buried in one of the mountains of Moab, and *no man knoweth his grave to this day.* Content with having left the law to the people, he sought oblivion for himself as far as possible.

Now, after four thousand years of waiting, after the performance of numberless prodigies, after His resurrection from the dead, our Lord willed that His tomb should be exposed to the veneration of the universe for all future time. This tomb became the shrine of holy pilgrimage for nineteen centuries, and the swords of Europe and Asia disputed its possession for ages.

Because one single prediction—that of Malachias—distinguished the Baptist, John wrought no miracle in behalf of the multitudes whom the reputation of his sanctity had gathered about him on the banks of the Jordan. But he declared himself unworthy to perform the humblest office for the Son of God. If our Lord is not God He manifested less zeal for the divine honor than Moses or the Baptist or the saints. Not content with declaring Himself equal to the Father, He affirms that *all the works wrought by God are His works also.* No prophet ever spoke in this manner. Instead of giving glory to God for every good and perfect gift, Jesus Christ attributes them to Himself as their author.

The Old Law was delivered on Sinai and was

there sanctioned ; the New Law was sanctioned on Mount Thabor. Accompanied by Peter,
James, and John, our Lord ascended the mountain. His face shone like the sun and His garments became white as snow. There appeared
Moses and Elias, speaking to Him on the excesses which He would suffer in Jerusalem.
Heaven institutes the comparison, and the mission of Jesus Christ is put to the test. If not
true it becomes obligatory on the Most High
to admonish the trembling disciples that this
Jesus is only His envoy, lest we may fall into
error, and especially, when resplendent in glory,
both the law and the prophets bear Him testimony in the persons of their greatest representatives.

In the former instance, when the meek son of
Amram was summoned to the mount, God treated with him as His servant and ambassador.
Lest Israel, terrified on the plain, should mistake Moses for God descended upon earth, the
Lord, in a voice of thunder that rent the rocks
of the desert, proclaimed : *I am who am, and
none but me shall you adore.* Moses came down
bearing between his hands the law written on
two tablets, and he presented it ministerially to
the people for their acceptance.

All nations to the day of doom are gathered

in spirit round Thabor and hear the sanction.
Every eye is looking, every ear is listening, all
hearts are throbbing. Jesus Christ is presented,
not as the minister, but as the Son of God—
Himself the legislator and the author of the
law. No command is given Him. One with
the Father, He is presented to all mankind as
Himself the supreme and eternal law. *This is
my beloved Son: hear Him* (Luke ix.)

If from Thabor we pass over to Calvary, where
all His indignities were completed, it is no less
the theatre of His glory and the vindication of
His divinity. Here were fulfilled all prophecies,
all truth was manifested, all miracles were renewed, and all the attributes of the Almighty
displayed. The cross, the instrument of shame,
became the chair of doctrine, the throne of the
eternal and ever-blessed Trinity. All the universe mourned and it felt the shock to its centre when its Author hung dying and bleeding
on the cross. The sun was darkened, the earth
trembled, the dead arose, the veil of the Temple
was rent from top to bottom. All things proclaimed that it was no mere mortal man that
perished on that mountain.

His omnipotence is manifested more by His
action on the souls of men than even by all the
external wonders. He instantly converts the

most obdurate and heartless sinners. One was
a death bed conversion—a dying malefactor, who
had lived all his life without God and was blas-
pheming almost to his last breath. The other
was an infidel, a gentleman, a scholar, and a Roman officer, educated, like men of his rank, in
the first schools in Rome or Athens, and sneer-
ing at all religions with the growing philosophy
of the former reign—a reign when religious sentiment and morals perished in the empire and left
an outward decency only. VERE HIC FILIUS
DEI ERAT, exclaimed the centurion. The third
conversion was, if possible, more miraculous still.
It was that of the mob who had poured out from
the purlieus of the city to witness a public execution—three of them—which had the fascination
of the circus and of the gladiatorial combats for
the sweltering rabble. *And all the multitude
of them that were come together to that sight,
and saw the things that were done, returned
striking their breasts* (Luke xxiii. 48). The
conversion of one sinner is a greater work than
the creation of the world.

Many just and holy men had borne testimony
to the truth by the shedding of their blood.
Human elevation, less than even obscurity, is
no shield against the sufferings that always accompany virtue and merit, and they are the

portion of the saints on earth. From Abel to
Zacharias many had died for righteousness'
sake. Nature silently wept over their wrongs,
waiting patiently for the day of final retribu-
tion. Now, for the first time, the forgotten dead
indignantly started from their time-worn tombs
and reproached the living for the dread God-
man. The world had perpetrated its enormous
sin : it had crucified its Creator!

To atone for our sins, and to repair the dishonor cast on God, Jesus bowed His head in
death. Because of the union of the human
and divine natures in the person of Christ all
that pertains to God belongs to Him, and all
that is peculiar to Him as man must be asserted of God. God was born for us, He suffered for us, and He died for us. For Jesus
Christ is infinite and eternal : He is God. Was
the faith of the penitent thief inferior to that
of Abraham? *Blessed are they who will not be
scandalized in me.*

But death was soon compelled to yield the
victory and acknowledge the glorious triumph
of our Lord. On the third day He rose again
by his own power, as had been foretold by
Himself and by the prophets. The seal of Tiberius, the Roman empire, could not prevent it ;
and Tiberius himself had the honesty to con-

fess it, desiring to enroll Jesus Christ among the Roman gods. Jesus rose, not as Lazarus and others, who had been resuscitated by external power and soon returned to the grave—Jesus Christ arose as the author and principle of life, to die no more. What had never been granted to man He possessed—immortality on earth. For forty days He conversed with His apostles, ate and drank with them, as he had done previously.

By the same inherent power He ascended into heaven without external aid. No angel, no fiery chariot is there, as in the case of Elias. Received into His eternal empire by the heavenly host, He despatches two of the celestial messengers to console His mourning disciples, and to promise them and us that at another day He will come in the same manner in which we saw Him depart.

The ascent of Elias from Horeb was witnessed only by the prophet Eliseus, lest any one not so well instructed might believe him to be God. Jesus Christ ascended in the presence of five hundred disciples, who accompany Him with their homage and their sorrows at His departure. A termination so sublime to a life of surpassing greatness would immortalize idolatry and utterly destroy all religion, if our Lord was .not God—especially at a time when men worshipped impostors and the legislators whom the fancy of the poets immortalized for the purpose of flattering the people by persuading them that Heaven had sanctioned their acts and their laws.

Jesus Christ is true God and true man—a fact taught by the Church at all times and for nineteen centuries, under the sword of the persecutors, and in witness of which many millions of her children died in all manner of torments. The Eternal Father, the Holy Ghost, the angels, the patriarchs, the prophets, the apostles, the saints, the living and the dead, the unclean spirits, the universe, all nature, establish this grand and astounding mystery beyond the reach of rational doubt. Lost to all sense of shame and human reason must be he who is capable of denying so authentic a fact—a fact which civilization and the very name of Christianity so plainly establish.

As living members of Jesus Christ we also were predicted with Him and are made sharers of His supreme dominion over all creatures. A Christian is superior to nature; all things are subject to him, for he is subject to God only. All a Christian's good works are, in a sense, miraculous, for they spring from a principle superior to nature and to human weakness.

We, then, must be miraculous—masters of the world by despising it, elevated above nature's laws by subduing them, arbiters of our destiny by submitting to the will of God, stronger than death by desiring it, to be united with our head, Christ Jesus. Look over the face of the Church in all ages; look at her pontiffs, her martyrs, confessors, and virgins, her missionaries, her religious orders, all the saints, the poor ennobled by their poverty, all the good of the world—they are the creation of Jesus Christ. Great must He be who has exalted the weakness of human nature to such unearthly perfections.

Therefore our Lord and Saviour Jesus Christ is the true and only Son of God, born of the Father before all ages, consubstantial with Him and perfectly equal to Him in all things, one and the same God, and the Second Person of the holy Trinity.

CONFERENCE IV.

ON THE DIVINITY OF OUR LORD JESUS CHRIST,
THE SECOND PERSON OF THE BLESSED TRI-
NITY (CONTINUED).

The moral Teaching of our Lord harmonizes with Man's three great
Relations—Its Establishment proves its Author to be God—
Paul and Barnabas taken for Gods—Precepts, Maxims, Coun-
sels, Parables of our Lord are all divine—The true Portrait of
Virtue—Benevolence of our Lord—His absolute Holiness of
Life—He weeps—Judas and Pilate—His heroic Virtue—His
Miracles, certain, public, and numerous, confirmed by His Ene-
mies—Perpetuated—One sufficient—Prove all Catholic Faith
—His Favors, Promises, Gifts, all divine—He sends the di-
vine Paraclete—Gives Power to remit Sins, to work Miracles
—Promises the conversion of Nations, the Perpetuity of the
Church, the Infallibility of the Pope—Apologists gloried when
charged with adoring a crucified God—Christ's second Coming—The last Day—Moral Reflections—The Sacred Humanity—Hypostatic Union the Wonder of Eternity—Worthy of supreme Worship—Excellence of the sacred Humanity—The
Temple of God—Perfect Work of the Holy Ghost—Sanctuary
of the Blessed Trinity—His Soul a perfect Mirror of God—
Always saw the divine Essence—Knowledge infused and acquired—All pertaining to God belongs to Jesus Christ—God is
born, suffers, and dies—Jesus Christ is infinite—He is God.

I.

There hath stood one in the midst of you whom you know not.—
JOHN i. 26.

MY BRETHREN :

When I last addressed you I proved how
splendidly the divinity of our Lord is established by the external glories of His ministry.

To-day let us dwell on that spirit of His divinity which embraces His doctrines, His favors, and His promises, and on the miracles by which these are confirmed; all and each equally prove that Jesus Christ is true God.

Our Lord's moral teachings and the manner in which these teachings were announced and confirmed unquestionably prove His divinity. They regulate man's relations to his Maker, to himself, and to his fellow-beings. And His precepts are so perfectly in harmony with these relations that their superhuman adaptation proves their author to be the Creator and Sovereign Lord of man and of all things.

Man is bound to love God, his neighbor, and himself in a reasonable manner. The moral code of Jesus Christ inculcates and regulates these loves in the most perfect way. *Thou shalt love the Lord thy God with thy whole heart and thy whole soul, with all thy strength, and with all thy mind.* This love accords with the idea which both reason and faith give of the great First Cause. He must be loved for His own sake as God, and then on account of the excellence of His being. He is the absolute good, whom we are destined to possess for ever, and He has lavished upon us all that He possesses. Our love for Him must be a loyal love, firm and true, and superior to the most rude and violent assaults.

Thou shalt love thy neighbor as thyself. We are instructed by our Lord to love not only our parents, friends, and benefactors, but every human being as we love ourselves; because all are made to the image and likeness of God, or have been redeemed by the precious Blood, and are our brothers. For this reason our Lord wills that we should pray for all and in the name of all. *Our Father who art in heaven*—thus shall you pray. We must do our neighbor no injury, inflict no pain, and, in short, we must do unto him as we would be done by; and we must pardon the greatest injuries.

We must love ourselves—not with a disorderly self-love, which is the greatest enemy of God and man. To know how to govern this love is essentially necessary for our present and future happiness; this important lesson our Lord has taught us.

We are commanded to love the soul more than the body, because it is more excellent and more like God. The body is to be loved for the end for which it was bestowed, as an instrument to practise virtue and obtain merit. Man must despise the life of the body when he can preserve it at the loss only of the soul.

10

We are made for society, and each has the same relation to the community that one member has to his body, while society has the same relation to the individual that the body has to each member. Every individual is commanded by our Lord to prefer the general good to his own private interests. *Render therefore to Cæsar the things that are Cæsar's.* We are also united among ourselves by the bonds of religion. Man is bound to sacrifice, when necessary, all his temporal goods, and even his life, for the preservation of society and the salvation of any one of his fellow-beings. *This is my commandment, that you love one another, as I have loved you.* Our Lord loved all men in general, and each in particular, so far as to die for the salvation of each. He has, therefore, set us the example, which we are under the obligation of imitating when necessary.

Such are a few of the sublime teachings of the Gospel of Jesus Christ. They have won the admiration of adversaries. "I confess," says one, "that the simplicity of the Scriptures amazes me and that the sanctity of the Gospel speaks to my heart." How paltry all the wisdom and learning of the philosophers when compared with them! We must conclude that the moral code of Jesus Christ places man in his true relation to his Creator, to himself, and to his fellow-man. It is in harmony with the designs of God in forming us. It is divine, and its author must be God.

In the Gospel all is adapted to the wants and high destiny of man, worthy of sound philosophy and reason, inspiring a contempt for perishable things and a love for those that are eternal. All contribute to the peace and happiness of society. He places the reward of virtue in the honor of obeying God, who will be its future recompense. He recommends the approbation of a good conscience to all human applause. He prefers God before man, eternity before time, and the soul before the body. He teaches that prosperity is mostly an evil, elevation a giddy precipice, glory a vain bubble, afflictions real blessings, the earth an exile, and all that ends with time a vain dream.

Language like this revolutionized the world, astounded philosophy, and caused an entire people to believe the disciples gods for having used it in their preaching.

All our Lord's precepts bespeak His divinity. The commandment of loving our neighbor goes no higher than that of loving Him as ourselves; but the obligation of loving Jesus Christ goes immensely farther, for it requires us to love Him as God and above all things. *He that loveth father or mother more than me, is not worthy of me; and he that loveth son or daughter more than me, is not worthy of me* (Matt. **x**. 37).

Rather than sacrifice the love we owe Jesus Christ we must be willing to give up all that we hold most dear in this world, and even life itself. Now, could our Lord ask so absolute a sacrifice if He were not the source and cause of the same and greater goods? Could He claim our life if He was not the author and disposer of it? No; it is the prerogative of God alone, from whom we have received our being and every other good. Jesus Christ is, therefore, God. It would be impious to sacrifice to a mere creature our whole being, life itself, destined to confess the power and dominion of the Supreme Architect who called it from nothing.

Jesus Christ requires, as a last mark of His love, that we should die for His sake and shed the last drop of blood in the heart rather than abandon Him. *Fear ye not them that kill the body. He that shall lose his life for me shall find it.* If He is not God, can there be among civilized nations a being so stupid as to be seduced by such impiety? Could a doctrine

so monstrous have confounded all pagan philosophy, subdued all sects, prevailed over all
human wisdom and learning, and triumphed
over the universe?

Human sacrifices are an abomination. We
justly deem all the nations barbarous that im-
molate themselves and their offspring to impious idols. But can any higher distinction be
claimed for the millions of Christian martyrs
who died for the sake of our Lord under every
excess and variety of torture? The Stephens,
the Vincents, the Sebastians, and indeed the
legions of martyrs who washed their garments
in the blood of the Lamb rather than bend
the knee before an impious idol, only ex-
changed one species of idolatry for another!
The generous confessors of the faith, who
braved tyrants and rushed into torments rather
than deny the holy name of Jesus, were but
brainless fanatics! And the tyrants themselves
who shed the blood of the saints, instead of
having been the enemies were the benefactors
of our race and the true saints! In that case
Christianity is but an impious sect, the world
is deceived, and the blood of the martyrs, instead of being the seed of virtue, has deluged
the world with idolatry, superstition, and vice!
If not consumed by the worm and moth, the

old bones of Herod, Tiberius, and Nero would rattle in their graves, if they knew the honors conferred on them by the philosophers of these latter ages. Nothing can more effectually check impiety than to exhibit it to its own gaze in all its native absurdity.

The manner in which our Lord announced His doctrines proves His divinity. His words are of superhuman wisdom. What truth, calmness, and simplicity in His counsels! *Watch and pray, for ye know not when the time is.*

His maxims are all wisdom; their bare enunciation leads the mind captive, and the world has adopted them as principles so simple as to lie within the reach of the most ordinary capacity, and so sublime as to have won the admiration of the most profound thinkers. *Where thy treasure is, there is thy heart also. Sufficient for the day is the evil thereof.*

Mark the wisdom of His parables. The conception is beautiful, the narrative unaffected, the moral simple. God only knows how many poor sinners have wept over the parable of the prodigal son. Can anything be more encouraging than that of the father of the household? How wide the difference between them and those of ancient and modern times! They were compiled to amuse and depict the absurdities of man, and they sneered at his follies; their morals are mostly pernicious and corrupt, and at best only frivolous. In all His parables our Lord not only instructs but He compassionates; and when He attacks men's vices it is only for the purpose of healing them.

The enemies of our Lord frequently attempted to entrap Him in His answers to captious questions, that they might be able to construe His words into a crime. Behold His calmness, His promptness, and the infinite wisdom by which He not only extricates Himself, but entangles them in the very meshes they had astutely prepared for Him. *He that is without sin among you, let him first cast a stone*, was His answer to the Pharisees who brought before Him a woman taken in adultery, that He might pass sentence on her. *Render to Cæsar the things that are Cæsar's, and to God the things that are God's*, was His answer to the Herodians who came maliciously to ask Him if it were lawful to pay tribute to Cæsar. This answer covered His enemies with shame, but they were not irritated with Him; for not He but the truth alone confounded them.

A divine eloquence and an irresistible power of persuasion prevail throughout all His exhortation; so prompt and indeliberate is our assent that each seems the spontaneous production of our own reason. Hear how He instructs man to have recourse with confidence to God in his wants and necessities: *Which of you, if he ask his father bread, will he give him a stone? or a fish, will he for a fish give him a serpent? If you then being evil, know how to give good gifts to your children, how much more will your Father from heaven give the good Spirit to them that ask Him?* Is not this the way in which the man who is God should vindicate His attributes before men? His every expression is overflowing with infinite wisdom; every sentence is a rich mine, which remains unexhausted although worked for nineteen centuries. All is true, all is sublime, all is wise; the purest reason is conspicuous throughout. Nothing can be added and nothing taken away, for it is a masterpiece of Him who does nothing except what is perfect.

Our Lord's teachings are enforced by the sanctity of His life. If the most learned man attempt to paint virtue, unless he has the type in his own soul and is good himself, his picture will be a distortion, like the writings of all the philosophers of former and recent times. They are a mixture of good and evil, radiant with beauties and teeming with deformities. Men

write themselves, and they cannot give a portrait of virtue, for the model is not within them.
Our Lord gives us the true idea of sanctity, for
He was its type and form. His reason was never
clouded by ignorance nor His heart disturbed by
passion. He was perfectly wise, and therefore
perfectly holy. From His first appearance we
are amazed at His sanctity. He is conspicuous
for the primary virtues—the love of God and
man—the foundation of all holiness.

What dependence on God's will, what zeal for
His glory ! Never yet did being love his fellow-man with a love so pure, so sincere, and so
disinterested. With what zeal does He not
instruct, with what benevolence does He not
aid, with what patience does He not support
them ! He possessed nothing, He claimed nothing ; He refused the crown that was offered
Him. He was never seen to smile, but He often
wept over man's misfortunes. He always pray-
ed, always labored, never grew remiss. How
humble His demeanor, how holy His conver-
sation, how innocent His life ! He challenged
even the Pharisees to prove Him guilty of the
slightest fault. On the other hand, how noble
were His sentiments and how elevated above all
that is deemed desirous by men ! How benevo-
lent and tender was His care for the poor, the
11

sick, and the afflicted ! Witness the number of the blind, the lame, the deaf, the sick, the mute who experienced the wonderful effects of His heavenly power as He passed among them.

Exempt from all the defects of nature, the familiarity even of the apostles served but to discover new abysses of holiness in Him. The sublimity of His intentions clothed His ordinary actions with so much sanctity that He is not less divine when He eats with the Pharisee than when He raises Lazarus from the dead. Holy must He be when the very disciple who betrayed him, and who had an interest in exposing his faults in order to conceal his own perfidy, paid public homage to His innocence. Even Pilate, when he condemned Him to death, in the very same breath declared Him just and sinless. No wonder the multitude demanded who this extraordinary being was whom the winds and waves obeyed. No wonder they called Him Jeremias, and others Elias, or some one, at any rate, of the prophets.

Virtue is truly heroic only when it combines both opposite extremes, as extreme patience and extreme zeal. There is nothing more difficult than to unite both extremes, and we rarely possess any virtue in an eminent degree unless at the cost of the opposite virtue. The most gentle is often timid, the most just hard and severe, the most prudent often cowardly. Jesus Christ always united both these extremes. If you desire examples of extreme goodness, extreme pity, extreme mildness, consider our Lord presiding at the judgment of the adulterous woman, conversing with the Samaritan at the well of Jacob, and apologizing to Simon the Pharisee for the sinful woman of his city, or inviting Himself to be the guest of Zacheus. In these instances we readily recognize the Father of the prodigal son and the Good Shepherd.

If we desire examples of extreme fortitude and freedom let us contemplate our Lord reproving the Scribes and Pharisees, reproaching them for their hypocrisy, their secret vices, their sacrilegious abuse of all deemed most holy in religion. No human considerations could check or weaken the intrepidity of His zeal. While perusing the Gospel you will meet many other instances to superadd, but none to contradict what I have adduced. Such, then, is Jesus Christ in announcing His sublime code of morals.

If our Lord was only an ambassador from heaven His mission could only be to preach to the gentiles the unity of God. To the Jews, who already possessed this true faith, His mission could be of no advantage. They had Moses and the prophets. If not God, in either case He not only failed but He defeated its object. The prophets never compared themselves to the Deity, but constantly announced that there was but one God. Our Lord declared Himself equal to the Father, confirmed the Jews in their belief regarding Himself, and denounced the denial of His divinity as blasphemy. Paul and Barnabas rent their garments when the Ephesians would venerate them as gods. The angel of the Apocalypse declined the relative homage of St. John? Had our Lord less zeal for the honor of God? If but a man, in claiming divine honors before and after His death His mission scandalized the Jews and buried the world in idolatry and superstition.

Of what advantage is His mission to the world if His followers are profane idolaters? Is, then, the advantage to be obtained by the advent of the Messias? Is this, then, that new Jerusalem foretold by the prophets, embracing countless hosts of every tribe and nation under the sun, and into which the kings and rulers of the earth would enter and adore the God of Israel in spirit and in truth? Is this, then, that fulness of grace and the Holy Ghost, the reign of everlasting holiness and peace, which the prophets foretold would accompany the advent of the Desired of all nations? Then this event so happy for man, promised from the foundation of the world, and so magnificently introduced, after four thousand years, as man's only and last resort, serves but to corrupt the world and bury it in a new and more universal idolatry! Into what an abyss do not human pride and reason fall when they raise themselves up against the Most High and attempt to sap the foundations of Christian faith and man's only hope for time and eternity!

From the consideration of the sublimity of our blessed Lord's moral teachings, the manner in which He announced them, His wisdom, and the sanctity of His life, let us now reflect on the manner in which he confirmed His doctrines and proved His divinity. This was accomplished chiefly by His miracles and promises.

A miracle is a work contrary to the laws of nature which none but God can perform, or one to whom God has given that power for the purpose of confirming the truth of declarations made in God's name. The sudden bringing on of any disorder or sickness, the instantaneous removal thereof without medicine, the raising of the dead to life, and such like, are miracles. They have been wrought by Jesus Christ, and by others in His name; there is as much evidence to prove them as to prove any other facts that took place in the past.

According to the dictate of reason and the common consent of the human race, miracles are incontestable evidences of truth. They are proof against the keenest criticism and they mark the hand of God. They are the undoubted seal of the Divinity in attestation of truth, the silent but powerful voice of the Omnipotent, at whose bidding all other arguments cease, because the voice of God is equally conclusive to all minds, of whatever state or condition.

II.

Whenever our Lord gives a precept He gives a corresponding grace to keep it. Whenever He inculcates great mysteries He proves them by the performance of great miracles.

Our Lord wrought miracles; there is nothing more sure under heaven. The Gospel narrative gives us the history of many. Let us select a few: at one time He feeds five thousand men with five loaves of bread; at another He changes water into wine; then He cures divers diseases, casts out unclean spirits, raises the dead to life; to show His glory He is transfigured on Mount Thabor; He raises Himself from the dead; after forty days He ascends into heaven ; He has but one human parent, who is at the same time a spotless virgin and a mother. These are some of His miracles, and there is nothing more certain.

What proofs do you require to be convinced of facts which you have not witnessed? That they should have taken place, not in a corner, but publicly and in broad day, in a civilized community, and that they should have been performed in the presence of many trustworthy witnesses ; and if these witnesses were of all ages and of every condition, so much the better. But our Lord's miracles were wrought in the most enlightened age of the world, the golden age of literature, and their publicity is a warrant against fraud and cunning.

What if their witnesses are even the declared enemies of Him who performs them, and if, despite of their malice, they admit them as incontestably true? In that case there is no possibility of mistake, and no sane man can doubt them. Such are our Lord's miracles.

Could anything occur more open, more visible, or more tangible than the raising of Lazarus to life close to the gates of Jerusalem, one of the most populous and enlightened cities in the universe? No less so was the curing of the man who was born blind, and whom everybody knew; the feeding of the multitudes with a few loaves and fishes; and the instant cure of many of all manner of diseases in the middle of the streets, and in all public places, and everywhere in the villages, and cities, and towns, and highways of Judea. The sun in the heavens is not more certain than these marvellous facts. These miracles bear the seal of the conviction of those who, enraged against our Lord, clamored for His death and attempted to prevent the miracles from becoming known, though truth forced themselves even to acknowledge them: *Non possumus negare.* The people who trail over the earth—the penalty of having rejected their Messias—confess that these miracles were wrought among them by One who preached the most sublime doctrines, which He confirmed by all these wonders; that He styled Himself King of the Jews, Christ, and the natural Son of God; and they confess that for these reasons they put Him to death. Do we need any further authority to convince us of the truth of these miracles?

The manner in which they were performed removes all doubt regarding their veracity. Every circumstance forbids the suspicion of human agency or contrivance. They were wrought without preparation and without physical or me-

chanical appliance, at any and every moment,
everywhere, and by a single word. This is the
only art, the only medicine ; at this single word,
and sometimes without a word at all, the blind
see, the lame walk, all the multitudes are suddenly
cured of their infirmities. *Lazarus, come
forth !* Like the creative fiat, at this sound
the festering body of the dead awakes to life,
and the multitude confess that such works were
never before seen in Israel. The Jews determined
to destroy both Lazarus and Jesus, God
and His witness, because they could not deny
the miracle. Oh ! the blindness of the sinner's
heart.

Although His miracles display the divine attributes
of goodness and compassion for His
creatures, our Lord did not perform them from
motives of mere benevolence, for the same reasons
exist to-day to cause Him to banish pain
and death from the world. He wrought them for
the higher purpose of establishing the truth of
His teachings, and especially that He is God.
We all share in them ; they are perpetuated in
the Church, and each proves every point singly
and the entire body of her doctrines.

When the Baptist sent his disciples to inquire
if Christ was God, for their answer He performed
many miracles in their presence, and added : *Go*

and relate to John what you have heard and seen : the blind see, the lame walk, the lepers are cleansed, the deaf hear, the dead arise again. This was in accordance with the prophecy of Isaias.

After Jesus had cured the man who was born blind the chief men among the Jews waited on Him and asked Him to tell them openly if He were Christ, or God—for both meant the same thing. He answered: *The works which I work in the name of my Father, they give testimony of me.* Before He raised Lazarus to life He declared formally that He performed the miracle that those who saw it might recognize Him as the sent of God.

To resume: God alone could give power to perform these miracles. This none can deny. It is equally clear that an individual exercising this power in proof of facts which he announces gives abundant evidence that God is with him, that what he declares in the name of God must be received as true ; for God becomes responsible for the truth of His declarations. That our Lord performed miracles no sane man can deny ; then God was with Him and all that He spoke is true. He wrought His miracles to prove His divinity ; God would not permit the performance of a miracle for the purpose of establishing a lie, thus making Himself the witness of a falsehood, to the detriment of His own honor and glory and of our salvation. Nor would the Spirit of God instruct the prophets so as to dispose the minds of men to believe a falsehood. Nor would He inspire the Evangelists to write a romance for the practice of mankind to the world's end. It follows that Jesus Christ is the true and only Son of God, is equal to the Father, and perfectly like Him; He is God, and the Second Person of the blessed Trinity.

Whom do you say that I am? demanded our Lord of the apostles. Peter answered in the name of the rest: *Thou art Christ, the Son of the living God* (Matt. xvi.) Our Lord puts us the same question to-day. We answer: *We know and we believe that thou art the Christ, the Son of the living God.* We pray to hear the same words addressed to us as to Peter as the reward of our faith: *Blessed art thou, Simon Bar-Jona.* Yes, with this faith we are happy in this life, and will be happier still in the life to come.

Man or angel could never recount the mercies of Jesus Christ to the human race. He has bestowed on us law, order, society, art, and science—the world itself and all it contains. He took away the sins of the whole world, opened the way to heaven, made us children of God and heirs to His eternal empire. Seated at the right hand of God, His gifts still flow with unabated abundance. He pardons our sins, nourishes us with His body and blood, makes us members of the true Church ; He heals our infirmities, consoles our sorrows, and is with us in our journey to the grave. To use His own divine words, He is our way, our truth, our light, our life, our salvation, and our justice.

"Favors make gods" was a maxim of pagan times. Man's worship is the expression of his love and gratitude towards his benefactor. Men, forgetful of their Maker, worshipped the air by by which they lived, the sun that gave them light by day, the moon and stars by night, the conquerors who saved them from their enemies, the wise princes whose just laws made them happy and contented. The benefits bestowed by the best benefactors of our race are paltry when compared to the favors conferred by our Lord on every tribe and nation and individual in the universe. Constituted as man is, there cannot be wanting on earth those who will adore Him, thank Him, and bless His holy name.

He does not end His miraculous life by instructing His disciples to thank God for every good and perfect gift conferred through His ministry. On the contrary, before He bids farewell to earth He binds us to Him by ties both indissoluble and everlasting. He commands us to believe in Him, to hope in Him, and to love Him still. He promises more than He had already bestowed, and assures us in His own words: *I am with you all days, even to the consummation of the world.*

The favors bestowed and the promises made by our Lord prove Him to be God, for they are such as none but God could make and accomplish. In number, in extent, and in their application they surpass the favors already bestowed.

He promises to send His disciples another Comforter, who proceeds from the Father, to teach them all truth and to abide with them for ever (John xvi.) What power had He over the Spirit of God, if that Spirit was not His own Spirit also? He fulfilled this promise ten days after His ascension by sending down the Holy Ghost on the day of Pentecost. This is the Spirit of truth, which the world cannot receive; the Spirit of peace, of consolation, of fortitude, to give strength to the martyrs, zeal to the confessors, piety to the entire world, light to guide and direct the pastors of the Church which He animates. He has changed the entire face of the world and has created a new earth. He forms

the saints, confounds incredulity, confirms the
faithful, converts sinners, and supports us all in
our trials and sufferings.

He promised to give His priesthood the power
of forgiving sins—a power peculiar to God alone.
The Jews were scandalized when He asserted this
power for Himself. Great is the astonishment of
the world when we read that on the day of Pentecost He bestowed on man, weak man, this
identical power which He had of remitting sins
(John xxi.)

An amazing test of truth was the promise to
give His apostles power to work miracles in His
name, which, without rashness, none but God
could promise or effectually bestow. The apostles displayed that power in testimony of His
divinity. Not in the name of Moses but in the
name of God did Josue command the sun not to
go down towards Gabaon while He was combat-
ing for the people of God. But it was in the
holy name of Jesus that the apostles raised the
dead and cured all kinds of diseases instantly,
and it was in that name that they converted nations. Without its influence they were as pow-
erless as Moses without his rod. So infinite
is Jesus Christ that the grave, where all human
power and greatness ends and is buried in the
dust, was the cradle, was like the morning star

that ushered in the empire of His omnipotence and of His everlasting reign.

He promised them the conversion of the world, the triumph of His cross over all nations, the universal sway of His kingdom ; and that princes and kings, that every nation and tribe and people, should adore Him in spirit and in truth in His one true Church. If He did not hold in His hands the hearts of all men, how could He promise or effectually cause a revolution never before witnessed ?

He promises that upon Peter, as upon a rock, He will build His Church—that is, the congregation of the faithful—and that *the gates of hell shall not prevail against it.* Such a promise includes a divine power, not only of converting the hearts of men and drawing them by the unity of faith into the one fold, but of securing to them the integrity of that faith and its government against all the powers of Satan. This promise was made good when our Lord commanded Peter *to feed His lambs and His sheep* (John xxi.) This congregation of believers, under one supreme pastor, then began, and it continues to the present day under one head, our Holy Father, Leo XIII. (whom may God long preserve!), the successor of St. Peter and the vicar of Jesus Christ on earth. This is the

Catholic Church, *the pillar and ground of truth* (1 Tim. iii. 15).

She is the infallible witness of the divinity of her Founder, carrying His name, His doctrines, and His precious blood all the world over. Her system is so perfect that not a single point of her faith could be effaced without a shock to the entire body or without marring the beauty and harmony of her unearthly symmetry. As there can be but one true God, there can be but one true faith (Eph.)

From her foundation, the Church of God has experienced the most violent assaults from persecutions, heresies, scandals, from the wickedness of all mankind, and from the immorality of many of her own children. But nothing has been able to shake her from the rock on which she was built by her divine Master. The most powerful dynasties have disappeared and are no more, earthly kingdoms and empires vanish, but the kingdom of Jesus Christ is a kingdom of all ages. The Lord is faithful to His promises: *Heaven and earth shall pass away, but my words shall not pass away* (Mark xiii.)

Take away this faith and you destroy the Christianity, the civilization, and the happiness of the world, and you leave man as aimless as the savage in the desert or as vile as the Mohammedan in his harem.

Paganism reproached the early Christians for adoring a crucified God. Our famous apologists triumphantly refuted all the calumnies of the times uttered against the faith. But in this fact of the cross they gloried, and in this they vindicated the divinity of our Lord, by their writings, their virtues, their sufferings, and their death.

Although always present with us in His marvellous Eucharistic life, our Lord will come again a second time as we saw Him leave us at Olivet. He will come in power and majesty in the clouds of heaven, accompanied with all His angels and saints, to judge the living and the dead. He is Alpha and Omega, the beginning and the end. Every eye ever quenched in death shall see Him, every ear shall hear His voice, every tribe of the earth shall receive, trembling before His throne, the sentence of their everlasting doom. Abraham, Elias and the prophets, all the patriarchs, the apostles and martyrs and saints, all the renowned men of the world, good and bad, all the humble and the great of Adam's race, and all the angels of heaven will adore Him as the arbiter of the fate of every human being, the Lord of life and death, the King of ages, the Prince of eternity, the Master of men and angels, the sovereign Judge of the universe. He is *the Lamb which was slain from the beginning*, and who *liveth for ever and ever*, who *redeemed us to God . . . out of every tribe, and tongue, and people, and nation.* He conquered *sin, and death, and hell.* He *led captivity captive ;* delivering us *from the power of darkness*, and acquiring for Himself *a name* above *every name that is named*, the only name *under heaven given to men whereby we must be saved.* And at *the name of Jesus every knee* shall *bow, of those that are in heaven, on earth, and under the earth*, and *every tongue* shall *confess that the Lord Jesus Christ is in the glory of God the Father.*

The union of the divine and human natures in the person of our Lord does not destroy but perfects His humanity. He is true man. This union intensified all his susceptibilities of pain or pleasure in a manner inconceivable to us. We must love Him not only as God but as man, and adore His sacred humanity with supreme worship and for many reasons.

The body of our Lord is the temple of God, in which all the plenitude of the Godhead dwells (Col. ii. 9). It is the most perfect work of the Holy Ghost, formed from the virgin blood of the Immaculate Mother, and especially made for the purpose of suffering, as the eye is made to see. It is the treasury of all miracles, of infinite graces and merits; it is the sanctuary of the Blessed Trinity and of all divine perfections, so that He is called in Holy Writ *the Holy of holies, magnificent in holiness and holiness itself.* As man he is the meet dwelling-place of the divine Word, in whose formation the Father displayed His power, the Son His wisdom, and the Holy Ghost His sanctity.

As first-born from the dead and head of the Church triumphant in heaven, the beauty of our Lord's body surpasses the combined splendors of all angels and saints and all creations. Multitudes felt no hunger for days while feasting on the beauty of His mortal countenance; the disciples fell into ecstasy on Thabor, where they could have remained for ever contented with one glance of His glory. The angels long to see Him now in glory; the seraphs are never satiated with the vision. The sight of Him is the beatific vision, and the loss of Him is hell. He is the delight and the complacency of the Father (Matt. iii. 17).

Nothing can be compared to the splendors of the human soul of our omnipotent Saviour. To say that it surpasses the combined splendors of all the hosts of heaven is like saying that the earth is larger than a grain of mustard-seed. His memory is the image of the living God and the mirror of the divine perfections uninterruptedly contemplating them. In His understanding he saw from the first instant of His creation God, the Blessed Trinity, the divine essence, and all His infinite attributes openly and face to face. In God, as in a bright mirror, he saw all things, past and present and future. No thought was ever conceived, no word spoken, no creature ever exists which he does not know. He knows all actual and possible things in creation, and His science as man is limited by the infinite possibility only in the Creator.

His will is the unbroken exercise of all virtues in the highest degree, and it is a perfect image of the divine will. His soul is adorned in the most eminent degree with all virtues, with the gifts of the Holy Ghost, and with all graces. In fine, as man Jesus Christ is an immense ocean of all prerogatives, excellences, graces, and virtues. His humanity merits the supreme adoration of angels and saints, and of all creatures, and is worthy of all love on account of its union with the Word.

Be astonished, O ye heavens, . . . and, ye gates thereof, be very desolate. Our Lord is not loved by His own creatures, whom He created, for whom He died on the cross, and for whom He is all inflamed with love.

Remember that He who loves us is the Son of God, the Creator and sovereign Lord of all things, and that man is but dust and ashes, sin and misery, whom the Lord needs not. His love for the least of us surpasses the combined love of all the angels for the Blessed Trinity, and all created love, even instinctive, united on one object. It is greater than our Lord's love for Himself. He has given us all He possessed as man—His labors, His honor, and His life; He endured shame, contempt, and the dreadful torments of the Crucifixion for each individual.

His love is so infinite that He has nothing; and there is nothing in Him which He has not bestowed upon us, even His very body and blood. Let us make a return by keeping His commandments, and they are not heavy. With justice did St. Paul exclaim: *If any man love not our Lord Jesus Christ, let him be anathema, Maran Atha* (1 Cor. xvi. 22).

CONFERENCE V.

ON THE DIVINITY AND PROCESSION OF GOD THE HOLY GHOST, THE THIRD PERSON OF THE MOST HOLY AND UNDIVIDED TRINITY.

The Holy Ghost is God—Sins forgiven, the Sacraments administered, and the Gospel preached in His Name also—The Sign of the Cross the most succinct Creed—Communication a Necessity of God—Inward and External—The Paraclete a Necessity—Proceeds from the Father and the Son both—Sanctification attributed to Him—A Person, not a separate God—Creates Order—Harmonizes and perfects Creation—Perfects Redemption—Creates the Humanity of Christ —Inaugurates His Mission—The Word the Prophet and Precursor of the Holy Spirit—His Descent—The living Soul of the Church—Possesses all absolute Perfections—Governs the Church—Presides at General Councils—The Pope His Infallible Organ—No Christianity if He is not God or forsook the Church—His Graces, Sacraments, Gifts, Fruits— The indelible Character—The three unrepeatable Sacraments —The Sin against the Holy Ghost—Redemption fruitless unless applied by the Holy Ghost—Apostasy—Moral Considerations, etc., etc.

I.

I believe in God. . . . And in the Holy Ghost, the Lord and Giver of life, who proceeds from the Father and the Son, who is adored together with the Father and the Son, who spoke by the prophets.—NICENE CREED.

MY BRETHREN :

There is but one God, and there can be no more. He is a shoreless ocean of divine being, and His nature is incomprehensible to created mind. He exists in an adorable Trinity of three distinct Persons, the Father, and the Son, and the Holy Ghost. They are not three Gods, but one, having one and the same incommunicable nature equally, the same identical attributes, and only the personality proper, though virtually in each.

No human learning nor science could discover this profound secret of God's manner of existence, nor could fathom its depths when known. In the providence of God four thousand years had elapsed before the world was sufficiently prepared to receive the adorable mystery. Typified, indeed, by all creation, and intimated in Holy Writ from the first page, it was reserved for no less a harbinger than the Man-God to remove the veil and to exhibit to the universe the full face of the Deity in the splendors of His being, and at a time when reason and philosophy were in the zenith of their power and glory.

When the Word made flesh hung naked and bleeding on the cross it was meet that type and figure should cease, and that the Blessed Trinity should manifest Himself in unclouded majesty, and that revelation should be perfected; all which were accomplished by the mission of the Holy Ghost.

The divinity of the Holy Ghost is taught by

the constant tradition of the Church and the
clearest texts of Scripture commissioning His
apostles. Our Lord commanded them to go and
teach all nations, baptizing them in the NAME
—not names, to show the unity of nature in
the Deity—*of the Father, and of the Son, and of
the Holy Ghost.* Now, none of them can be a
creature, as was falsely asserted by the Mace-
donians formerly, and more recently by Socinus
and infidels. Sins are remitted in baptism; only
God can forgive sins—each Person is equally
God. *There are three who give testimony in heaven, the Father, the Word, and the Holy Ghost.
And these three are one* (1 John v. 7).

Language cannot express the faith of the
Church more distinctly. There never was a belief more formally professed from the beginning
of the Christian era, in all places and at all times.
Millions of times daily the miraculous symbol is
written on the face of the multitudinous hosts of
the Church, from the rising to the going down of
the sun, in making the sign of the cross in the
name of the Father, and of the Son, and of the
Holy Ghost. Impiety may scoff, incredulity
may ridicule, and heresy sneer at this *abridged
creed* embracing implicitly all revelation; but
we know it is the sign of the Son of man, the
banner of the heavenly hosts, the assertion of the

divine existence and the wisdom that has revolutionized the world, converted the nations, and civilized the human race.

The doctrine of the Blessed Trinity is not opposed to human reason, but above it. It is not a question of abstract reasoning but of pure evidence. It has been revealed to us by our Creator, who is essential truth and must be believed with unhesitating conviction, as He must be loved unreservedly as the supreme good.

All the investigations and reasoning of ages have evidently demonstrated that there is no contradiction between science and revelation. God is most simple and pure, without combination of parts, either material or spiritual, and without distinction between will and performance—A SIMPLE ACT. His nature is a plenitude, or, as a doctor has it, "a super-fulness of perfection," like the good measure overflowing and spilling on all sides.

Communication is a necessity of excellence. The divine nature must communicate itself eternally. This communication is double—one internal and not free, because a condition of God's existence, without it He would not be God; the other communication is external and free, as the creation. It may or may not be, as God wills. The perfection of the divine nature is infinite,

18

and the natural and necessary communication of it is also infinite. It must communicate itself in its fulness and without multiplying itself, because infinity cannot be multiplied. Hence the fecundity of the divine nature in three adorable Persons.

The Father is the fountain of the Godhead, the Son His knowledge of Himself, the Holy Ghost His love of Himself—one essence in three equal divine Persons. The Father must necessarily generate the Son, the Son must necessarily be generated. They must necessarily love one another; it mingles, is ever breathed forth, and the Holy Ghost is ever breathed forth by necessity, or proceeds from both because of the infinite plenitude of the divine nature. There can be no inequality, no diminution, no priority in this ineffable communication of itself. Then God exists in three divine Persons, who are really distinct and equal in all things, are uncreated and eternal.

Because they are inseparable in nature all external or free acts are produced by the Blessed Trinity combined.

However, some works are more especially attributed to one rather than to another, because of its relation to that Person. Thus creation is attributed to the Father, redemption to the Son, and sanctification to the Holy Ghost.

By a person is meant a free, intelligent, and independent agent, as man. The Holy Ghost is the Third Person of the Blessed Trinity, distinct from the Father and the Son, but not a separate God, but one and the same, having the same nature and perfections, and equal in all things with them. The name is not essentially peculiar to this adorable Person, for each is a spirit, and holy, and God; it is given Him by the Church and in the Scriptures, because He is breathed forth from both as one principle, and not by way of generation, like the Son, but by way of procession; and this, having no parallel in creation, cannot be adequately expressed in earthly language.

Many Christians do not correctly understand what they rightly believe and is plainly taught by the Catholic Church in regard to the Holy Ghost, and this is detrimental to the spiritual life and is unworthy of the divine honor. The Holy Ghost is not an adjunct of the Deity. He is the Spirit-Creator of the world, the ever-blessed God from everlasting, all God's love, the form of the Blessed Trinity by whom we know, love, and serve our Creator, our Redeemer, and Himself, the One True God in the undivided Trinity.

The universe is a material image of God, the

written book in whose pages all can read His holy name more plainly than in all the volumes of human science. Creation manifests the Almighty Father, the world His unbegotten Son, its order and preservation the Holy Ghost, and who in external acts, as in the Blessed Trinity, is the perfection of His ways. He is this divinely instinctive attraction or charity which rules supreme, binds all the elements of creation in unbroken harmony, systematizes all things, and impels the worlds in their course through the realms of space.

In the beginning God created heaven and earth, . . . but *darkness was upon the face of the deep.* The crude mass was informal and wild, and its jarring elements in boisterous strife, until the Holy Ghost moved over the abyss, issued firm laws, and bade disorder cease, when fair creation sprang forth, proclaiming the power and wisdom of Him who made it. *Send forth thy Spirit, and they shall be created,* says the Psalmist (ciii.) And again Ecclesiasticus (i. 9) declares that it was by the Holy Ghost that God created the wisdom that governs the universe.

Man, the intermediate link between matter and spirit, is still a more perfect image of God in his soul. He is a spirit and immortal, intelligent and capable of knowing and loving his Maker.

In his body he is organic matter, and in his whole nature united to the Word by the Incarnation. In this second, wonderful stride in creation the same creative energy and co-operation of the Third Person are conspicuously manifested. But in the order of grace and in our redemption the action of the Holy Ghost fills the soul with love and wonder.

All the astounding mysteries of religion, the unknown and hidden things of the divine wisdom, and the secrets of eternity are revealed to us by the Spirit of love, mild and gentle and sweet as the dove, His material image. I can readily conceive the astonishment of the evangelist at the answer of the Corinthians to St. Paul when he asked them if they had received the Holy Ghost. They did not know if there was a Holy Ghost. The reproach will apply to many who do not realize their faith and cherish a more tender devotion to our Lover and the Spouse of the soul, God the Holy Ghost. An abundant harvest of grace and many consolations would assuredly reward the devotion.

The price of our redemption was paid by the Second Person, but it was applied only by the Third Person, otherwise it would have remained barren and ineffectual, and would only have irritated our wounds the more and made our sad condition more desperate.   For centuries had we languished at the fountain of Bethsaida, and no friendly hand was found to help us to plunge into the healing waters. God had taken two· steps towards us—the first by creation and the second in redemption. He must take a third step and come still nigher to us. We need God the Holy Ghost to lift us up, enlighten our souls by faith, strengthen us by hope, and purify us by love—the promises made through the prophet Joel (ii. 28): *I will pour out my Spirit upon all flesh.* According to the vision of Ezechiel the entire world is a wilderness of dead men's bones. They shall be created anew ; they shall live again.

In the work of our redemption the victim is prepared by the Holy Ghost. How can this be ? asked the chaste spouse Mary. The Angel Gabriel answered that the mystery would be wrought by the Holy Ghost. He *shall come upon thee, and the power of the Most High shall overshadow thee* (Luke i. 35). The Third Person created the human nature of our Lord and all His faculties as man—a fact proclaimed thrice daily by the tongue of the Angelus bell all the world over as the sun tells his shining hours : "The angel of the Lord declared unto Mary, and she conceived of the Holy

Ghost." Sublime mystery! and announced to the world as plainly as the starry hosts of night proclaim the might of God.

Our blessed Lord's journey to Calvary may be traced by His blood; no less marked are the steps of the Holy Ghost in His divine co-operation. Our Saviour grew from infancy to manhood like an ordinary man, and until His thirtieth year the prodigies that clustered about Him were apparently produced by outward agency. An angel admonishes the shepherds, directs the flight into Egypt, a wondrous star conducts the kings from the remote East to Bethlehem, and all Judea and Jerusalem are in consternation.

Now another point is reached and a new era begins in His life, inaugurated by the Holy Ghost. The Father promises the Baptist a sign from heaven by which he will infallibly know that Christ is the Messias : *He upon whom thou shalt see the Spirit descending and remaining upon Him* . . . adore; *this is the Son of God* (John i. 33, 34). True, His humanity was created in the chaste womb of the Immaculate Virgin by the Holy Ghost, but hitherto He seemed to be separated from it externally. Now He takes solemn and visible possession of this marvellous temple of God in the form of the dove and at His baptism—the new birth in its Christian institution.

The public ministry of our Lord begins; no longer does the current of His life steal quietly on in the sequestered vale of Nazareth, but it is manifested to all mankind and is directed towards Jerusalem.

That His mission may be the more definitely marked and His co-operation in the work of our redemption more specifically pointed out the Holy Ghost did not descend while Christ remained on earth. Could the human mind conceive a greater advantage than the visible and permanent presence of Christ on earth until the last day ? Would not all doubts be removed, all difficulties solved, sin and error be put away, and the earth become the paradise of God ? Greater advantages will accrue from the descent of the Holy Ghost, and in order to obtain them it is to our advantage that our Lord should leave the world. *It is expedient to you that I go ; for if I go not the Paraclete will not come to you.*

Moses and the prophets announced the advent of the Son of God, but Jesus Christ is by excellence the prophet of the Holy Ghost. The Baptist was the precursor of our Lord, but our Lord is the precursor of the Holy Ghost. But He not only promises Him ; He prepares the way for His coming by the shedding of His Most Precious Blood for our redemption. He instructs His disciples how they are to prepare themselves to receive Him in a becoming manner. They are not to depart from Jerusalem; they must withdraw from all intercourse with the world, and in recollection and prayer be ready for the accomplishment of the mystery of the descent and indwelling of the Third Person in the Church, which He will animate as the soul does the body, lead into all truth, vivify, purify, strengthen, and in which He will abide till time shall be no more.

Our Lord's teachings must be supplemented, a channel must be instituted for their presentation and communication to all men. Like the body of Adam before receiving the breath of life, the body of the Church was materially fashioned, but not till the day of Pentecost did it receive a living soul—the Holy Ghost. Hence her doctrines are the veritable teachings of God; her worship, her laws, her discipline, her ceremonies, all divine. Wilful disobedience to her authority is disobedience to God and her chief in the chair of Peter, the infallible teacher of all mankind in the way of salvation. The absolute perfections of the Holy Ghost, His self-subsistence, His action on the Church and on the souls of the faith-

ful, are all plainly taught by Holy Writ.   I
select a few passages from many :

*I will ask the Father, says our Lord, and He
shall give you another Paraclete, that He may
abide with you for ever, . . . the Spirit of truth.
. . . He will teach you all things, and bring all
things to your mind, whatever I shall have said
to you. . . . Whom I will send you from the
Father. . . . Who proceedeth from the Father. . . . I have yet many things to say to
you, but you cannot bear them now. But when
He, the Spirit of truth, is come He will teach you
all truth. . . . He shall receive of mine and
shall show it to you* (John **xiv. xv.** *et seq.*)

The Holy Ghost is not an energy nor a detached grace or gift, but the Adorable Majesty of
heaven. *They were all filled with the Holy
Ghost, and they began to speak with divers
tongues, according as the Holy Ghost gave them
to speak* (Acts ii. 4).   This He did not as an inspiration but as a Person.   He directs Peter to go
to Cornelius, and commands Saul and Barnabas
to be set apart for the ministry (Acts **x.** 26).

From this divine Person is derived the mission
and authority of the apostles and their successors, the bishops, to instruct, to rule, and to
govern the Church of God to the end of time
(Acts **xx.** 18).

Revelation, foreknowledge, the personal knowledge of all the hidden things of God, sanctification, the bestowal of all divine gifts, and all that is claimed for the Father and the Son are equally asserted by the pages of inspiration for the Holy Ghost, for THESE THREE ARE ONE.

It hath seemed good to the Holy Ghost and to us, was the announcement made by the apostles, through the mouth of St. Peter, at the Council of Jerusalem, and which must be held of all the general councils of the Church for nineteen centuries. The doctrinal teachings of all the successors of the Prince of the Apostles during that long period and for all future times are the very teachings of God the Holy Ghost, thus verifying the declaration of the prophet, that *all thy children shall be taught of the Lord.*

II.

On the day of Pentecost the Holy Ghost descended on the apostles in the form of tongues of fire and became the living soul of the Catholic Church ; and He will animate it for all time, carrying the grace of redemption to every human being. Otherwise Christ's promises failed and Christianity perished with His last breath on the cross. When did He abandon His mystic Body, His Spouse and Church? The visi-

ble descent of the Holy Ghost on the Church
was solemnized by many of the wonders that
always attested the manifestation of the majesty
of God to our race. The voice of nature is
heard: the thunder and lightning of Sinai, the
splendors of Thabor, the earthquakes of Golgotha, are all renewed with a greater still, in order
to rebuke the impiety that denies to God the
power to remain with us under the appearance
of bread. He comes down under the appearance
of tongues of fire.

In the mystery of the Incarnation Christ entered into the bosom of the Blessed Mother only.
He did not take possession of each of us individually. He assumed our nature, but not our
person; He is my brother, but He is not I. He
bequeathed His humanity and divinity under
the form of bread and wine, and thus loved us
to the term of His possibility.

We have no adequate idea of the extent of
the ruin wrought within us by original sin and
our own personal transgressions. A new creation alone can remedy all our evils and re-
store us to our pristine soundness. The royal
prophet uttered the petition of humanity when
he exclaimed: *Send forth Thy Spirit, and they
shall be created; and Thou shalt renew the face
of the earth* (Ps. ciii. 30).

This second and more perfect creation is wrought by the Holy Ghost. Mark well the narrative of the Gospel: *And there appeared to them parted tongues, as it were of fire, and it sat upon every one of them* (Acts ii. 3). He descends on each individually and dwells in each, making of the very body *the temple of the Holy Ghost.* Without assuming our nature or person, he unites Himself with us by an ineffable union, not only indwelling but purifying, enlightening, changing, deifying in a manner by His grace, which is a participation of the divine nature. In the language of the apostle, He creates a new man, who henceforward will beam and be inflamed with the love of God and of his fellow-man ; his heart will be a deep over which the Spirit of God now reigns, and whose purified waters not all the worlds ever created could contain. Only the shoreless ocean of God's existence can hold them.

Witness the transformation of the apostles, the pillars of the new heaven and the new earth. Although for years in the company of the God-Man and sharers in His power, they were timid, worldly-minded, almost without faith, without love, without perseverance, attached to God externally, but severed from Him in mind and heart. No sooner do they receive the Holy

Ghost than they are superior to the combined powers of the world and hell. The gentiles mistake them for gods.

You may as reasonably attempt to count the sands on the sea-shore or the stars of heaven as our saints, whom none can number. Each is the tabernacle of the Holy Ghost. The persecutions of the world-wide Roman Empire, armed with flames, and the sword, and the rack, and the wild beasts, could not subdue the fortitude of a maiden in her teens nor of a hoary pontiff tottering under the weight of years. Ye millions of martyrs, of virgins, of confessors, of priests and bishops, of monks and hermits, and ye countless hosts of the laity—hidden saints—I hail you as the new creation, the most perfect work of the Omnipotent Trinity, the cloud of witnesses proving that our Lord's word has not failed—that the Holy Ghost has not forsaken His Church, but *will abide with* her *for ever.* As truly as the person of Christ is perpetuated in the Blessed Eucharist the Holy Ghost is conferred by confirmation as really as He descended on the apostles and was imparted by them to the faithful, but without the miraculous signs, for the reason that miracles are not the special gifts of the Holy Ghost and were performed by the disciples before the day of Pentecost.

The gift of miracles is for others and makes no alteration in the soul of the possessor, but is dangerous to his humility. The seed of the Word, they are intended chiefly for one class of unbelievers—those who have no other means of learning the truths of religion. To those who believe, they are generally useless and are calculated to diminish the merit of faith. For the enlightened, who can ascertain the truth of the miracles recorded in Scripture, they are superfluous, and also for those who fall away from the faith. The standing miracle in proof of religion is the miraculous preservation of the Catholic Church for nineteen centuries despite the combined powers of earth and Satan. If the evidences of belief were not conclusive its rejection could not exclude from heaven and condemn one to everlasting flames.

It is by grace that the Holy Ghost acts on the soul. It is a supernatural gift gratuitously bestowed for our salvation, and without which, if abandoned to our own natural efforts, we could no more reach heaven than the fiend or the beast of the field, even though as learned as the philosopher and endowed with all the natural virtues of which man is capable in his most civilized condition. *Without me you can do nothing*, says our Lord.

Though easily defined, not the brightest intellect can comprehend the stupendous gift of sanctifying grace. Its manner of existence, its incessant operations under the impulses of actual grace, the perfect freedom of the will under its almost omnipotent influence, neither St. Paul nor St. Augustine could unravel.

As we breathe the air that surrounds the earth, so do we live in the atmosphere of grace and inhale its incessant inspirations. God alone can tell the number of graces given to each individual according to his state, disposition, and condition in life. To confess one's sins to a priest, to pardon an injury, to resist a temptation are supernatural acts which created energy cannot produce. Each requires a mission of the Holy Ghost, an indwelling of God. It is Himself, and not His gifts separately, that is bestowed.

The infinite gulf between God and man is bridged over; and though at times, especially in seasons of sorrow and suffering, vehement showers of grace are rained on us, each is a greater work than the millions of worlds which illumine the firmament at night. Each additional degree is worth more than the universe. St. Joseph, to whom is accredited the forfeited primacy of the fallen chief of heaven's hosts, might willingly descend from his brilliant throne and taste over again all his old sorrows, in order to obtain the merit of giving one cup of water to the least deserving of the human race.

God is honored by the receiving of His favors, and in this He has fixed His outward glory. As He could not create a being capable of comprehending the Deity, or, in other words, as it is impossible for Him to make us Gods by nature, He has made us Gods by grace, says a profound theologian, enabling us to possess with Him the same beatitude, the same kingdom, and the same end. *You are Gods, and all of you the sons of the Most High*, said the Psalmist. *The kingdom of God is within you*, said our Lord. "The soul of the just is the throne of God," exclaims St. Augustine.

The miraculous gift is best known by its effects ; these are twofold—a proneness to good or a concupiscence which inclines the will to embrace virtue, to love and practise purity and honor and truth and all virtues, to prepare for death and be always ready to meet the summons to eternal rest and peace. Next divine grace instils into the soul an aversion for evil—an aversion not only for the impiety that stalks boldly through the land and shocks decency by its notoriety and excesses, but an aversion also

14 `

for every infraction of the divine law, even in thought. Such is the operation of divine grace, and its result is a peace which the world cannot give nor destroy. The sinner cannot possess it; it belongs to virtue alone. It consoles under all adversities; the tears of the penitent inebriate with gladness; the lash cheered the confessors, and the martyrs sang hymns of joy when their flesh was burnt and their bones broken. These are the waters springing into eternal life, and with which the Holy Ghost inebriates every man who obeys His voice and forsakes the madness of sin, in which is shame, remorse, and perpetual death. Although gratuitously given, it is in our power to increase or diminish our graces in proportion as we obey or reject their inspirations; which explains the progressive sanctification of the virtuous and the perversity of the wicked.

While the sinner lives he is in the order of nature and of grace, and in this respect chiefly does his state differ from the damned. If his sins were as numerous as the sands of the sea and were of the most malignant type, if he obey the first inspiration he can bring down another and another still, and so on until he reaches the highest perfection, like St. Paul and like countless numbers of holy penitents in every state in human life. No limits are appointed, and it is not certain that any saint but the Blessed Virgin corresponded to the measure of graces bestowed. Woe to those who reject graces habitually and resist the Holy Ghost! Their certain inheritance will be the malediction of the faithless house of Israel, whose desolation will last for ever.

Though grace in general combines all classifications, there are mysterious and special gifts imparted to us by the Third Person which claim our deepest gratitude. In baptism He plants in the soul seven mysterious powers which contain the possibilities of the highest sanctity—infused habits which so exalt us that the transformation is called a new birth. We are *born again* (John iii.); we become *the new man*.

These supernatural habits are Faith, Hope, and Charity. They are called theological because they rest on God as their primary object, and they are the foundation of the moral virtues, especially of Prudence, Temperance, Justice, and Fortitude, which regulate all our relations to God, towards our fellow-men and ourselves, under all the circumstances incidental to our weary journey to the tomb.

The human soul, unspeakably a more perfect work than all the universe, is adorned by the divine Paraclete with His noblest gifts. Though the habits of virtue infused by Baptism can elevate it to the most exalted perfection, occasions may arise when a more prompt obedience, deeper comforts, and a stronger energy become necessary. In Confirmation, by means of which, by fixed covenant, God the Holy Ghost is imparted, He confers seven extraordinary graces or gifts to meet every emergency and co-ordinate with the infused habits or possibilities. These are : Wisdom—not that of earth, but that by which we prefer eternity before time, virtue to vice, life rather than death, God and His kingdom in preference to Satan and hell. Second, Understanding, by which the learned and the illiterate, the young. and the old, and all alike know the truths of religion on the same grounds of conviction—the authority of the Church ; outside of it there is only darkness and the shadow of death. Third, Counsel, the grace of the intellect dictating what must be done in each particular event, and instructing those in authority how to direct others. Fourth, Fortitude, a superhuman power, clothing the most timid with a strength which not the violence of temptation, the allurements of sensual pleasures, the hatred and persecutions, or more still the flattery, of the world can shake. It is the grace of final perseverance. Fifth, Knowledge — not of the mysteries of iniquity, of cunning and deceit, nor how to become wealthy ; but the knowledge of God, of the truths of salvation, of the mysteries hidden in the bosom of the Blessed Trinity from everlasting—the knowledge of ourselves and of *Jesus Christ*, and *Him crucified.* Sixth, Piety, the foundation of the spiritual edifice and necessary for all. It has promises for this life and for the next, and gives their full value to the other gifts, shedding around the sweet odor of good works. It bids the weary head rest on the bosom of God, the true Father, whose tenderness infinitely surpasses the combined compassions and paternities of the human race. Seventh, the Fear of the Lord, which is the beginning of all wisdom, the germ of all virtues, which steadies us in the path of duty. It teaches us to despise the fear of man, who is impotent to inflict any real evil, to avoid sin as the only misfortune, and to keep God's commandments. It takes us by the hand at our cradle, conducts us safely through the perils of life, and only parts with us when we are laid to rest under the cold clod of the valley.

Such are the marvellous gifts that adorn this new man and more perfect creation, making the soul the delight of God, on which He sits us on

a throne, establishes a kingdom that will never
end, and where He, with His angels and saints,
reign for ever and ever. Nothing in the universe
can match its beauty. The Holy Ghost sings
songs of jubilee over His magnificent work. He
compares its outward lineaments to the lilies on
the margin of the waters, to the flowers of roses
in the days of spring, to sweet-smelling incense
burning in the fire, to the cedars of Libanus
towering upwards until they reach the clouds.

Unlike the barren fig-tree, its branches are
bending with golden fruit. The Church counts
twelve, each of which has generalities and
would require volumes to describe. I will
merely glance at each. Charity—all the virtues of the just and the heroic perfection of the
saints come under this single classification.
Joy—in possessing the supreme Good and all
His infinite perfections. Peace—in the assurance that we can never be deprived of the object of our love and happiness. Patience—to
endure the storms and trials that will surely
assail the best and most holy. Longanimity—
the heroism of expectation for the unclouded
vision of God. Benignity—towards our suffering brother. Mildness—to pardon his tres-
passes against us. Faith—firm and active in
our heavenly Father and in all His teachings.

Modesty—in order to curb the gross tendencies of our inferior nature. Chastity—to subdue and restrain even lawful enjoyments within due bounds to prevent their becoming hurtful by abuse.

Such are the marvellous works of the Holy Ghost. In this manner does He apply to each soul the mercy of our redemption, renders grace as ubiquitous as the air we breathe, and with it almost deifying the human race.

Thus shall every man be *blessed . . . that feareth the Lord ; . . . glory and wealth shall be in his house, and his justice remaineth for ever and ever*, and *he shall be in everlasting remembrance* (Ps. cxi.)

Although grace and every other gift, internal and external, are the combined operation of the three Persons, yet the propriety of the Person is plainly marked on each. The physical world is a transcript of the Father, the intellectual world an image of the Son, and the moral, the world of will and love, the likeness of the co-equal Limit of the Godhead, the Third Person of the Blessed Trinity. Yet they are not three worlds, but one.

The seven Sacraments, perennial fountains of covenanted grace inundating the whole world like the rivers of paradise, are all under the power of the Holy Ghost, and are applied by Him to every child of God. Three—Baptism, Confirmation, and Holy Orders—confer the Third Person, and the two latter especially, and are marked with the seal of His dread sanctity. They cannot be repeated. Penance can wash away the guilt incurred by a violation of the obligations they impose, but they must not be repeated without incurring the guilt of sacrilege, the greatest of all sins. They imprint on the soul an indelible seal or mark—the name of Jehovah written in the blood of Jesus Christ, which can never be effaced. No, not all the iniquities of the world can blot it out, nor the unquenchable flames of the dread abyss burn nor the brightness of heaven outshine it. Like the sun, it will shine on for ever and ever, through weal or woe. Once ordained, a priest for ever; once baptized, baptized for ever; once confirmed, confirmed for ever.

To desecrate a church is a great impiety and is held in abhorrence by all civilized nations. How much greater the iniquity of a Christian who, by mortal sin, profanes both body and soul, the living temple of the Holy Ghost, and sets up the abomination of desolation in the holy place! The second paradise is laid waste. The prophet Jeremias, after exhausting the power of language, seizes on imagery to portray the dreadful ruin. She is the new and degraded daughter of Sion, whose desolation fills all the beholders with dismay as they clap their hands and exclaim: *Is this* Jerusalem *the city of perfect beauty, the joy of all the earth?* (Lam. ii. 15).

All sins can be forgiven except such as are of their own nature irremissible, such as obduracy in sin, final impenitence, obstinate heresy, despair. These are the principal sins against the Holy Ghost, and they *will not be forgiven, . . . neither in this world nor in the world to come.*

This assurance comes from God Himself. It is the sin unto death for which intercession is not to be made, according to the disciple of love. St. Paul says that the conversion of apostates is impossible. Here again is distinctly implied the mysterious impress of the Holy Ghost and the impiety of its desecration.

The sin against the Holy Ghost is irremissible. If we are amazed at the contemplation of His stupendous mercies, we are no less struck by this terrific menace. As the Holy Ghost is essentially love, the infinite, jubilant love of the Blessed Trinity, the very threat is a love; it is the expression of jealous and wounded

15

love, the assurance of the consequence of the persistent refusal of the mercy and forgiveness of the dove of the baptism, the ardent flame of Pentecost, and the despised Spouse of our souls, *who prays for us and in us with ineffable groanings.*

None of the nations that ever abandoned the Church have been reconverted. Few of the numbers, in our day or in former times, of the clergy or the laity who, like stars, fell from heaven and filled us with dismay at the depth of their fall, have ever been reconciled. Despite tears, and prayers, and menaces, they fell to rise no more and perished like Satan. They prove the correctness of the interpreters of the words of the Gospel, "that the terms imply not absolute impossibility but extreme difficulty, with but rare exceptions."

He that thinketh himself to stand, let him take heed lest he fall, is the admonition of the Holy Ghost. We all bear the grace of God in frail vessels. Admonished by the fall of an apostle, of the angels, and of millions of our race, let us not *sadden the Spirit of God within us,* but *with fear and trembling work out* our *salvation.*

May the sevenfold gifts, the precious graces, and rich fruits of the Holy Ghost strengthen us in the resolution to live faithful to His inspirations, to adore Him, to bless Him, and to thank Him! Let us always invoke His light in our doubts, His counsel in our difficulties, His strength in our conflicts with all the evils that assail us in this life of sorrow, until we see Him face to face in union with the Father and the Son, ONE GOD, for ever and ever. Amen.

CONFERENCE VI.

ON THE BLESSED TRINITY—ONE GOD IN THREE DIVINE PERSONS.

Mysteries in Everything—It is unreasonable to reject them—Definition of Faith—The Duty and Province of Reason—Faith not an Opinion—The Blessed Trinity and the Holy Eucharist—Consent of Nations—A Mystery an indirect Proof of Truth—Revelation an unbroken System—A Religion without Mysteries no Religion at all—A God like Ourselves—The pagan Idea—Faith the Reason of the supernatural Order—The Blessed Trinity proved by the Divinity of Christ—The Unity and Trinity—Abysses of Revelation—Its Simplicity the chief Reason of the Incomprehensibility of the divine Nature—Personal Relations—Correlative Relations—The Dogma proved—Tradition — Creeds — Liturgies—Prayers—Sacraments—Illustrations—Shadowed by all Things—Futile Objections—Impossible to be understood—Moral Reflections—Love of the Blessed Trinity for Man, etc.

I.

There are three who give testimony in heaven—the Father, the Word, and the Holy Ghost. And these three are one (1 JOHN v. 7).

MY BRETHREN :

The Blessed Trinity is so deep a mystery that not the combined intellect of angels and men, not even the soul of Jesus Christ, which embraces all creation within a glance, can comprehend it.

The prime 'article of our faith, we must embrace it with the full assent of our intellect and heart on the authority of God, who, through His Church, has been pleased to reveal to us His divine nature and the manner of His existence.

The Blessed Trinity means that there is but one God, and only one; that in Him there are Three divine Persons, who are distinct and equal to each other in all things; these Persons are the Father and the Son and the Holy Ghost. The Father is not the Son nor the Holy Ghost. The Son is not the Father nor the Holy Ghost. The Holy Ghost is not the Father nor the Son. The Father is God, the Son is God, the Holy Ghost is God; and they are not three Gods, but one God, because each has one and the same divine nature — not *partially*, but in its *fulness* and with all the divine attributes. The divine nature is infinitely simple and indivisible, and cannot be in parts.

A person means an intelligent, free, and independent principle of action, as man, with this difference, that in man it implies separation from every other; but there is no separation in God. Each possesses the Divinity undividedly.

The eternal generation of the Son and the

eternal procession of the Holy Ghost are the internal acts of the Deity, and are necessary, because without them God would not be one God ; He could not exist. In this they differ from the external acts, such as creation, which are free. The Blessed Trinity is one God. God the Father is the adored of the universal world, and the belief in Him is the happy necessity of reason. His assertion is almost an insult to the human race, and the denial degrades to the level of the brute.

Because it is a mystery and beyond our understanding some unhappy people refuse to believe in the Blessed Trinity. If man admits only what he can understand the circle of his information will be very limited. Mysteries of religion are truths revealed by God which we do not understand, but which we are bound to believe on the authority of God, and of His Church as the competent witness. When there is sufficient proof that God has spoken to us it would be the greatest impiety not to believe Him. For, not to believe Him implies that He could deceive us or be deceived Himself ; neither of which is possible, for He is essential truth.

To refuse to believe everything except what we understand is to contradict the laws of our nature and make the world a bedlam tenanted

by every descendant of Adam. We are sur-
rounded by mysteries of nature and by facts
which have never been explained. The production of all things from nothing; our body and
soul; the marvellous senses; every object in the
universe, both great and small, animate or in-
animate; the sun that rolls over our head, the
grain of sand at our feet, have secrets of existence never unravelled. Despite of analysis
and scientific classification they baffle our scrutiny, but are nevertheless true. Man is a mystery to himself. He who made us distinctly understands the wonderful machinery of the body;
the nature and essence of the soul are open to
His view. He is lifted above the heavens; He is
from eternity unto eternity; His eye beholds the
worlds that roll in harmony in the regions of
space. Man, a speck on a spot of creation, is
embarrassed in his inquiries into the simplest
object that dimly shows itself within the dark
labyrinth through which he journeys to the
tomb. Shall he make of his stunted little reason a magic wand, and boldly describe with it a
circle that Omnipotence shall not pass? He cannot explain the production from its seed of the
blade of grass on which he treads, nor can he
penetrate the properties of an atom of air which
he inhales; and yet he pretends to measure the

Infinite. Until he is acquainted with all the laws of nature in their mystic plans, and all the resources of Omnipotence, he dare not reject the truths taught by the Almighty because they are at variance with his limited notions of things.

Some persons pretend that there exists a discrepancy between what reason dictates and revelation teaches, as in this adorable truth. This arises from the fact that men draw their conclusions too hastily, and they conclude that they are well acquainted with what they but imperfectly know, and that reason testifies where it does not.

It is certain that God cannot err. Man frequently errs and is continually liable to mistakes. The history of the world presents us with an exhibition of the weakness of the human mind. Man is always adding to the stock of his information, abandoning former theories for new ideas, correcting his errors, and proving his imbecility while he asserts his strength. God is not so. Changeless amid a changing world, the heavens and the earth shall pass away, but His wisdom, His truth, and His word never shall pass away and are always the self-same.

But we are not compelled to accept as true a doctrine which we do not understand, unless there be sufficient evidence to prove that God revealed

it. Man has not been subjected by his Maker
to any dominion that could enthrall his intellect. The humblest individual is as independent in mind as the brightest seraph that stands
before the throne and glows in the rapture of
vision. A contrary course would be degrading
to man and unworthy of God. It cannot be a
religious duty to profess a falsehood: *Only the
truth shall make you free.*

Faith is not the abject slavery of the mind;
it is not opinion, it is not fanaticism, nor philosophy, nor irrational assent to unintelligible
propositions. Faith is a supernatural gift infused into the soul by which we firmly believe
all that God has taught on the authority of
the Church, *the pillar and ground of the truth.*
It is the root of all justice and has the same
relation to the supernatural that reason has to
the natural order. Faith is the dawn of the
beatific vision. It is a new mind which introduces us into the secrets of the world to come,
and it is the special gift of the Blessed Trinity.
The material object of this ineffable gift is the
entire body of all supernatural truths contained
in the Catholic Church and taught by her, in-
cluding her own divine authority.

As in nature, so too in religion, at every step
we hail a mystery—an abyss unfathomable to

our mind, but unquestionably true, and a knowledge of which is necessary for our present and future happiness. God, eternal, without beginning or end, and all things created from nothing; spirit and matter united in man; an angel rebels in heaven, and with all his legions is condemned to burn for ever in hell; the progenitor of our race sins—he and all his descendants are sentenced to suffer and to die; God becomes man, is born, lives visibly on earth for the space of thirty-three years; He suffers and dies on a cross between two thieves, leaves us His flesh and blood all over the world and for all times, and now sits at the right hand of the Father; He will come again and raise all the dead to life — all are abysses of unfathomable mercy, justice, and love.

These and all the doctrines of the Church, together with the ineffable mystery of the Blessed Trinity, are the subject-matter of divine faith and as true as God is in heaven.

We are as convinced of the existence of a future life, either of happiness or of torments, as we are of death, and of the truth of the doctrine of the Blessed Trinity as of the existence of the American continent. A temptation to doubt may arise, but a real doubt never touches any article of Catholic faith.

Although mysteries are incomprehensible, yet the evidences of their truth are so conclusive that no reasonable man can deny them. They are based on a chain of arguments and well-authenticated facts which are unanswerable. They are established by so many prophecies, so many and varied miracles, by the destiny and history of the entire world, by the unanimous voice of all mankind. All combine to authenticate a worship absolutely divine, that began with the world and will end with it—no, will last while God is God.

These divine truths and adorable mysteries mutually support each other, forming a system bearing the characteristics of truth and the seal of divine wisdom, majesty, and power. Whoever admits one, if he be consistent, must admit all. Whoever rejects one is as criminal as if he rejected all, for they are all founded on the same motives of credibility—the unerring authority of the true Church.

We are not allowed to look over the doctrines of revelation and reject those which do not seem to us as probable and rational; for that would be to believe on the authority of our own understanding, and this is not faith. The apparent contradiction of a doctrine to human reason or to a natural law is not the criterion of the truth of that doctrine. We often imagine there are difficulties in the doctrine when the difficulties exist only in our mode of conceiving it. The doctrine of the Blessed Trinity is one of pure evidence, and not one of philosophical scrutiny. It is certainly revealed by God and can contradict no principle of reason, but it is beyond the reach and domain of reason.

The incomprehensible depths of the mystery of the Blessed Trinity and of all other mysteries is evidence of their truth ; for a religion without mysteries is absurd, and common sense cannot receive it as divine. An attempt to underrate mysteries or to explain them away is an effort to lower the Supreme Being to our own level, and its logical end is pure infidelity. To say that the disclosure from an infinite to finite minds has no difficulties is a virtual denial of any such communication and it forfeits its character of being divine.

Our Creator is infinite in every sense ; nothing finite or created can reach Him. He could create a new and different world for every drop of rain that ever fell, and yet all would be only a speck in the shoreless ocean of His existence. What is infinite is incomprehensible to any height of created intellect. All things besides God are in a system. He is outside of all sys-

tems. To attribute to Him in their limited mea
sure our own faculties and attributes is to entan-
gle ourselves in contradictions and difficulties.
A God like ourselves is the pagan idea. We can
attribute to Him nothing except what is infinite.

The difference which separates God from us is
not like that which separates angels from men
or man from the lower animals; it is infinite.
When God condescends to make known to us His
nature, the manner of His existence, or any other
truth necessary for us to know, the incomprehensibility of this knowledge is the divine mark
of its truth. No explanation is made, no reason is given, from the fact that we could not
understand it. Hence He gave no explanation
when the Jews asked Him "how it was possible for Him to give us His flesh to eat."

All the saints who have ever lived could not
understand the "how can" in the Blessed Eucharist, in the Holy Trinity, nor in any other
mystery of religion. Faith alone can explain
and embrace them. Faith makes known to us
what the *eye hath not seen, nor ear heard*, and
what has not *entered into the heart of man*
(1 Cor. ii. 9). It is not the light of reason, but
the *great light* which outshines all, that ban-
ishes doubt and the shadows of death from the
mind, bathes the spirit in peace and in the joy of

divine conviction. Faith is the reason of eternal life ; without it *it is impossible to please God* (Heb. xi. 6).

The divinity of our Lord proves the doctrine of the Blessed Trinity. The special proofs of each are so obvious as to have convinced all civilized nations since the commencement of the Christian era. THESE THREE ARE ONE (1 John v. 7).

The most profound abysses of revelation are the unity and trinity of God—one as inaccessible to created understanding as the other. The oneness of God, His infinite simplicity, is the chief cause why it is impossible to comprehend the divine nature. Strictly speaking, He has no perfections. They are only our way of approximating to a correct idea of Him. He is Himself His sole perfection—the perfection of perfections. By this is meant that He possesses the plenitude of being without limitation, privation, or the dilution of possibility. Not only are all things possible in Him, but all possibilities are actual. He never has been able to be, He never will be able not to be. He simply is. Beginning, end, change do not touch Him.

"He is all things and He is nothing," says St. Dionysius, "because He does not belong to things at all." He is necessary and He is of

Himself. His illimitable being, and all His
infinite perfections, are blended in one—A SIM-
PLE ACT. All His attributes are concentrat-
ed on each other and become His substantial
qualifications—eternal love, infinite mercy, omnipotent justice. But they are justly distinguished by our minds because of the different
attitude in which the divine nature is placed
before us or considered in relation to esseity or
action. Thus we may contemplate the Blessed
Trinity in the profound solitude of His creatureless life or with creatures ; or the Son in the
bosom of His Father and in the bosom of His
Mother; or the divine Paraclete in the Father
and the Son and in the organism of the Catholic
Church. In the adorable, self-subsisting essence
of God there is no difference, no vicissitude of
change. This simplicity is marked on all His
works ; it is the character of truth, the secret of
all creation, the simplicity of plan constituting
the order and harmony of the universe and of
the Church.

What expression is to the human face this
simplicity is to the divine nature—its beauty
and its identity.

God, being the supreme and sovereign Lord,
can be but one. Two or more would be a contradiction, because none would be supreme, none

would be God—a truth established by unaided human reason. This fact was not questioned until after the Dispersion, when men had lost patriarchal traditions and the world was aging, and only distorted notions of revelation remained.

Virtue, civilization, true knowledge, and sound philosophy flow from the belief in the unity of the Deity. When abandoned for polytheism, and nearly every object and all vices were worshipped, a deluge of darkness, superstition, and crime swept over the face of the globe.

The Most High, in order that the human race should not perish here and hereafter, and that He might not be defeated by Satan in the object of creation, thundered forth the fundamental truth in the startled ear of mankind, whether in the stern glens of Sinai, the brickfields of the Nile, by the pyramids, or under the patriarch's tent. From among all the nations of the earth He selected one people, whom He made the guardian and depositary of this grand mystery and His other promises. The Holy Ghost inspired the prophets, who incessantly announced it by the swift waters of Babylon, amid the palaces of Jerusalem, or in the populous streets of gorgeous Ninive: *I alone am, and there is no other God besides me* (Deut. xxxii. 39).

This belief, without which salvation is ordinarily impossible, was not only taught in human language but indelibly written in type and sacrifice. There must be but one priesthood, one temple, one holy city, one altar, one sacrifice. It was exhibited still more perfectly in the Church, according to St. Paul: one Lord, one faith, and one baptism; one God, the Father of all (Eph. iv. 5). If, blinded by their passions and seduced by the surrounding nations, the chosen people at times staggered in their faith, they were again recalled to its profession by the most frightful chastisements.

II.

Lest it might be an occasion of idolatry to a people always prone to that crime, the mystery was only hinted obscurely from the beginning. It was said: *Let us make man to our image and likeness. . . . Behold, Adam is become as one of us* (Gen. i. 26; iii. 22). In many other places in the Old Testament the faith is more or less openly suggested. It was reserved for no less an envoy than the Son of God, the Second Person, to announce the plenitude of the divine nature to the world, lay the foundations of Christianity, and usher in religion in all its unclouded splendors.

Never was truth more clearly or solemnly promulgated than the doctrine of the Most Adorable Trinity on the banks of the Jordan. The Son is baptized, the Holy Ghost visibly descends in the form of a dove, and the voice of the Father is heard saying: *This is my beloved Son, in whom I am well pleased* (Matt. iii. 17).

There are three who give testimony in heaven, says the evangelist—*the Father, the Word, and the Holy Ghost. And* THESE THREE ARE ONE (1 John v. 7).

Frequently in the Gospel the mystery is announced in the most solemn manner, and always in the plural number and under the most striking circumstances. Invested with the same power and authority which He had from the Father, Christ commissions His apostles to announce this great truth to the world: *Going, therefore, teach ye all nations ; baptizing them in the name of the Father, and of the Son, and of the Holy Ghost* (Matt. xxviii. 19). *He that believeth and is baptized shall be saved; but he that believeth not shall be condemned* (Mark xvi. 16). St. Hilary, a Father of the fourth century, commenting on this passage, clearly expresses the doctrine of the Church in this manner: "They who possess in common the same nature bestow the same gift, for the name of the Trinity is God." *Believe you not*, said our Lord, *that I am in the Father, and the Father in me ?* (John xiv. 11). Commenting on this remarkable passage, St. Fulgentius says : "All the Father is in the Son and in the Holy Ghost, all the Son is in the Father and the Holy Ghost, all the Holy Ghost is in the Father and the Son."

It is unnecessary to multiply proofs. Invested with authority from above before their departure from Jerusalem, the apostles incorporated the divine doctrine in their Creed and made it the groundwork of all their teachings : "I believe in God, the Father Almighty, and in Jesus Christ, His only Son, our Lord ; I believe in the Holy Ghost." Their successors in the Church, inheriting their promises and clothed with their mission, have guarded the august mystery for nineteen hundred years, have taught it to the entire world, and will continue to teach it until time itself shall cease to run and the human race shall be gathered into its eternal home.

Whenever denied in any age the Church has always reaffirmed her doctrine by the decrees of general councils, explained it by the writings of her doctors, propagated it by the toil of her missionaries, honored it by the lives of her religious men and women, and illustrated it by the blood of millions of martyrs.

Every prayer, all rites and ceremonies, pious undertakings, good works, and all the operations of the religious life are begun and ended under the invocation of the august name, and for the simple reason that *the name of the Blessed Trinity is God.* It is in the name of the Father, and of the Son, and of the Holy Ghost that we are made children of God in Baptism, that we are made soldiers of Christ in Confirmation, ministers of religion in Holy Orders, indissolubly united in the Sacrament of Matrimony, and it is in this name our sins are forgiven in Penance.

In this holy name are all temptations subdued, the fiery darts of the most wicked one turned away, enemies conquered, dangers overcome, virtues acquired, prayers offered, petitions granted, and miracles wrought. Constantly holding the most profound mystery before our face while living, our most tender mother, the Church, bids the trembling soul depart in peace at the dread hour of death in its invocation : "Depart, O Christian soul ! out of this world, in the name of God the Father who created thee, in the name of God the Son who redeemed thee, and of God the Holy Ghost who sanctified thee." It is in · this omnipotent name that she commits to the earth, the common grave of all mankind, the cold remains of all her children who have died in peace. Invoked with the sign of the cross, this venerable name is the monogram of Christianity, the test of the true faith, and the banner of man's redemption. God knows Himself, else He would be ignorant ; He loves Himself, or He would not be holy. He is incessantly the subject of His own contemplation. This science of Himself never passes away or changes, and is a divine Person, consubstantial and eternal. This is the Father, the First Person, who thus knows and contemplates Himself.

He is called the Father because from this knowledge of His being and perfections is formed a full and perfect similitude of Himself, a real, subsisting person—the Son, consubstantial to the Father, and the Second Person.

The knowledge and contemplation of His infinite perfections is the bliss of the Father. It is mutual, and is returned in the self-same way by the Son. Love meets love. The act is consubstantial to both, because *all that is in God is God*. It produces the Holy Ghost, the Third Person, who is co-eternal and co-equal, the eternal bond of union, the limit of the Deity, and who proceeds from the Father and the Son as one principle.

The Blessed Trinity is God. Man, having
been made to the image and likeness of God,
illustrates in the three faculties of his soul the
august mystery. Our self-knowledge and our
affections, the operations of our understanding
and will, shadow forth the mystery, evanescent
in us, but in Him permanent and immutable.
The generation of the Son is produced by God's
knowledge of Himself; the procession of the
Holy Ghost by God's love of Himself—by the
love of both Persons united. It is the participation of this unspeakable mystery that constitutes the felicity of the saints in heaven ; its
adoration the consolation and dignity of the
Christian, his truth and worth, on earth.

Eminent divines show that everything in all
creation is an image of the Triune God. The
world shadows forth this astounding doctrine.
The free acts of God outside are a likeness of
the necessary acts of God within Himself.

All creation is, in a manner, a son of God—
a knowledge of Himself made manifest. It re-
flects His image and represents His perfections
so clearly that we are inexcusable if we do not
see God by the things that are made (Rom. i.
20). Preservation, which is only a going-on or
a continuation of creation or the creative act,
and distinct from it only in our conceptions—an

indivisible continuity—still more strikingly adumbrates the perpetual generation of the Son and the incessant procession of the Holy Ghost. The First Person is always and eternally generating the Son ; the Second Person is always and eternally being generated ; the Third Person is always and eternally being produced. This process must exist and never cease from all eternity, for God is an act, a simple act.

Creation, grace and glory, the Incarnation, the Blessed Eucharist, the beatific vision, all that we see around us, are the emblem of the Trinity in unity.

From its birth the sun simultaneously emits light and heat, exemplifying that even in nature there exist effects co-existent with their principle. The soul is simple and a spirit, yet it possesses three faculties—the memory, the understanding, and the will. In reasoning, the understanding soul is exercised ; in remembering, the recollecting soul ; and in loving, the willing soul. These are not three souls, but one with three distinct faculties, illustrating the adorable Trinity of Persons in the simplicity of the divine Unity, for " He made man to His own image and likeness."

While these illustrations do not pretend to unravel the unfathomable mystery, they nevertheless clearly prove, what the Church teaches, that this mystery is not contrary to but above and beyond reason. *As the heavens are exalted above the earth, so are* God's *ways exalted above* our *ways, and* His *thoughts above* our *thoughts* (Isaias lv. 9). *O the depth of the riches of the wisdom and of the knowledge of God! How incomprehensible are His judgments, and how unsearchable His ways!* (Rom. xi. 33).

All the sanctities of heaven are incapable of comprehending this august mystery; and after millions of ages passed in the enraptured contemplation its infinite ocean will remain unexplored. There remains the unknown life of the Blessed Trinity, whose waves never have broken on the shores of time. Faith supplies the defects of reason, and we unhesitatingly believe what it is impossible to understand on the authority of God's own word made known to us by His Church, the infallible teacher of the human race and *the pillar and ground of truth.*

Impiety in every form has assailed this most profound mystery; but its principal objections, as silly as they are impious, are directed alike against all religion, against the very being of our merciful Father, and even against natural truths and scientific facts.

The mysteries contained in a grain of sand have never been fathomed by man's intellect or explained by science. The last analysis of the raindrop baffles the skill of the chemist and scorns the tortures of his laboratory in the persistent efforts to extort its secrets. Based chiefly on a false interpretation of some verses of Holy Writ, a specific reply is not only not necessary, but would be an insult to good sense and to the settled convictions of our race.

I select one, not because I consider it important, but its apparent plausibility is calculated to impose on the unwary and unsuspecting non-Catholic, whose faith rests on human opinion only and is unprotected by the ægis of the Church. It is blasphemously asserted that the adorable mystery of the most Holy Trinity contradicts the vulgar axiom: "Things which are equal to the same or to a third are equal to one another," and there may be no distinction of persons. This paltry fallacy not only ignores but positively misstates the Catholic doctrine and does not apply at all to the question. It would force paganism on us; it creates three gods for our acceptance instead of the most HOLY ONE.

The divine nature is simple and indivisible. It is possessed totally, and not in part, by each

17

Person.   There are not three but only one God.
There is no third at all to which a comparison
can be made.   "The Father is eternal, the Son
is eternal, the Holy Ghost is eternal ; and they
are not three eternals, but one eternal.   The divine nature and all the attributes are common to
each adorable Person.   *Show us the Father, and
it is enough for us*, said the apostle.   Then our
Lord said to Philip :   *So long a time have I been
with you, and have you not known me ?   Philip,
he that seeth me seeth the Father also.*   And in
another place :   *The Father and I are one.*   The
personalities are not absolute perfections ; they
are most assuredly proper; they are relations of
ineffable tenderness, and are virtually possessed
by each divine Person.

In the divine communications that are inward
each imparts indivisibly and totally all Himself
without losing aught, while still retaining the
propriety of the personal relation.

Petavius, in his sublime *Tract on the Blessed
Trinity*, and other doctors who treat the great
mystery extensively, prove the essential absurdity of this objection and its fallacy in the sense in
which it is offered by infidel impiety.

We must ever remember that this ineffable
mystery is unquestionably taught us by the Almighty, that it is truth itself and the manner of

God's existence, and that it is impossible that He could exist in any other way.

It has stood the test of human reason and science for nineteen centuries of civilization, and has triumphed over the world. It has converted the nations, given a new and more vigorous impulse to science, literature, and art, banished the reign of idolatry, vice, and superstition. Like the sun in the heavens, it enlightens the universe and it can never perish; for the Blessed Trinity is God and His holy name.

Our divine Lord never undertook to explain this adorable mystery; no illustrations could reduce it to the grasp of created intellect, not excepting even the human soul of our divine Lord—how much less the angels of heaven! God alone knows Himself, and faith alone can comprehend Him; it is the light of His face shed on man's soul, and by which alone can we see or understand Him who *inhabiteth light inaccessible.*

The unbeliever will find humble and fervent prayer the shortest road to God and a most convincing proof. Let him ask our Lord Jesus Christ, who *enlighteneth every man that cometh into this world,* and who first announced to us in its fulness this adorable mystery. His prayer will not remain unanswered, for the promise is made.

It is our duty and our privilege to honor and adore the most adorable Trinity, to thank Him for making Himself known to us ; and for this knowledge, which *surpasses all human understanding*, we should practise all it inculcates, especially charity, the golden bond of union between God, ourselves, and our brethren, that we may see Him hereafter, face to face, whom we now believe and venerate on earth.

" Glory be to the Father, and to the Son, and to the Holy Ghost. As it was in the beginning, is now, and ever shall be, one God for ever and ever. Amen." This is the grand doxology of the Church, in which are gathered all her belief, all her love, all her adoration in the most succinct manner. Such is the termination of all her hymns, her psalms, and her canticles. The universal anthem resounds from age to age, uttered by the lips of all her children until silenced by the cold fingers of death. But the ransomed spirit resumes it in a higher state, and joins the heavenly hosts in singing it for evermore before the throne of the most holy and undivided Trinity.

Loving us as He does, there still exists a greater mystery than even the TRIUNE GOD— that His rational creature should not return His love, but refuse to serve Him and spurn His ser-

vice. I speak of a mystery in the moral order
—the mystery of sin and of a hard heart.

The Blessed Trinity created us and made us to
His own.likeness ; He has given us an immortal
soul and a body with its marvellous senses.
Heaven and earth, time and eternity, all He has
is ours—the Church, the angels and saints, the
sacraments, the Body and Blood of Christ Jesus ; in short, all He has and all He is belong
to His children, on condition that they accept
them.

Surely to reject God and turn away from the
end of one's creation must be an inconceivable
disorder. When man defeats the Blessed Trinity, sets himself up as his idol, adores some base
or paltry passion, and says, *I will not serve*, his
sin is great. Sweet Jesus, save us from the
dread impiety !

The Blessed Trinity is our Father and our Creator ; His very bosom is our home, and unless we
live there for ever our unhappy lot will be with
the hopelessly lost. Yet to make this sad choice
costs more than our salvation. The separation
from God is an ineffably great evil. If we have
sinned—and who has not sinned ?—let us return
to Him with confidence. He who sent His Son
to suffer and die for us will not reject us ; a
contrite and humble heart He will never despise ;

and even there is joy in heaven before the angels of God when the sinner repents of his sins.

Blessed be the MOST HOLY AND UNDIVIDED TRINITY, now and for evermore! Amen!

CONFERENCE VII.

ON CREATION, THE FIRST EXTERNAL WORK OF THE BLESSED TRINITY, AND ON HIS MOST JUST PROVIDENCE.

Creation God's first external Act—A Production from Nothing—Matter created in the Beginning and fashioned in Time—Not Eternal—Length of the six Days an open Question—The six Days' Work—Spontaneous Productions a Falsehood—Vegetable, Mineral, and Animal Kingdoms—The Creative Germ—Primitive Types unchanged—God and Providence—One and the Same—He governs all Things—Greatest in the Least—Agar and Ismael—Misfortunes—Inequality an Exaggeration—Small Difference between all Conditions—Suffering a Law—The Source of Moral Greatness—The Crucifixion and the Saints—Human Life a Point—Providence should be seen in its Totality—Moral Reflections—Man's Worth—Resignation to the Will of Providence—Conformity Man's noblest Sacrifice—Embraces all Virtues—Suits all Conditions—Source of all Happiness—Resignation in Small Things—Blessed Father Alphonsus Rodrigues, etc., etc.

He spoke, and they were made; He commanded, and they were created.—PSALM cxlviii. 4.

MY BRETHREN:

Creation is God's first free and external act. During eternity he dwelt in the creatureless solitude of the Blessed Trinity. The act did not increase His essential bliss. From benevolence, and a desire to possess children capable of knowing and loving Him and becoming sharers in His own happiness, He broke the everlasting silence of His reign, sounded the loud creative mandate, and by a simple act of His will called all things from nothing.

Like all external acts, it is the production of the Three Persons of the Blessed Trinity combined. Creation has always been a riddle to human learning and philosophy. The light of reason has never been able to explain the origin of the world; all the famous scholars of ancient times grossly erred on the subject, except Plato, who was acquainted, probably, with the sacred writings which furnished the most accurate information on the subject worthy of God and of man. Modern unbelievers labor to contradict the grand and simple narrative by renewing the exploded errors of pagan antiquity and adding others borrowed from every department of nature—errors of philosophy, errors of history, of anthology, of chronology. Nothing has been left undone to establish a contradiction between revelation and natural science on this great mystery, the first external word spoken by Jehovah. The theories of one generation are exploded by the next, and neither geology nor any other science has disproved a single statement in Holy Writ.

In the beginning God created heaven and earth (Gen. i. 1). This is the first and one of the greatest truths expressed in created language. It places the sacred Penman infinitely higher than all human science and systems.

The idea of creator is incomprehensible to the human mind. Pagan philosophy, which exhausted all the powers of reason, never reached it. Those great men who are justly admired by all generations for wisdom and learning traced the origin of the world to chaos, or primary and uncreated nature. They maintained that the divine energy organized this matter, but they were ignorant that it was itself created from nothing.

The heavens, although made simultaneously with the earth, seem to belong to a period anterior to the six days' work. We do not doubt that the sun, and the moon, and the stars were made before our time, and, indeed, before the time of man at all. "The universe, created in the beginning and before all time, was adorned and fashioned in time," says the learned Bossuet.

According to commentators, Moses uses the word to "create" or "produce from nothing" only in relation to this fact. It refers to the original production of all things from nothing in an inchoate condition. When describing God as organizing pre-existent matter and producing therefrom every variety of beings the sacred writer uses the word to "form" or "fashion."

The Hebrew word "Bara," to create from nothing, is always used in Holy Writ to designate creation in its strict sense. *I beseech thee, my son*, said the pious mother of the Machabees, *look upon heaven and earth, and all that is in them, and consider that God made them out of nothing* (ii. vii. 28). *In six days the Lord made heaven and earth, and the sea, and all things that are in them* (Exod. xx. 11).

To create properly means to give existence to things that did not exist previously—to produce from nothing. Such is the true idea of creation as furnished by all authentic sources of truth—by the Scriptures, the Creeds, the Fathers, the general councils, the popes, and by all reliable modes of teaching authorized by the Church.

The word "nothing," used in the definitions of the Church on this subject, is negative, in concontradiction to being or existence. It has never been used in a positive signification. "When a thing is said to be produced from nothing," says St. Thomas, "this means a relation or order, and not a material cause." The Vatican Council pronounces an anathema against any one "who denies that God created all things, and in all their substance, from nothing." It is of faith that the power to create belongs to God only, and that the world could be created and formed by Him only, the sole and efficient cause of all creation. *The Most High Omnipotent Creator is one God* (Gen.) *I am the Lord that make all things, that alone stretch out the heavens, that establish the earth* (Isaias xliv. 24). *God created all things* (Heb. iii.) To the Holy Scriptures is added the authority of the councils of Nice and Constantinople: "I believe in one God, maker of heaven and earth, and of all things visible and invisible." It is unnecessary to add the unanimous testimony of the Fathers on this important head. I will content myself with one unanswerable proof, furnished by human reason and selected from many others.

The world is limited, for it consists of limited parts, and therefore it is accidental, liable to change, and it is dependent. It must be the work of another, in matter and form, who is its co-efficient cause and produced it. What has been produced did not exist at a certain time and must have had a beginning, must have passed from possibility to existence. What is thus produced must have come from nothing, and consequently in time or at the beginning of

time. This plain argument refutes all impious
theories of unbelievers regarding creation. We
must admit that God created the world from nothing either in time or with it.

Creation clearly manifests the power and wisdom of God. The former is conspicuous in
the creation of matter, and the latter in the
beauty and forms into which it was subsequently
shaped.

The length of the six days is not decided.
The period of time during which the earth was
void and empty, and before the sun was created
on the fourth day, is an open question, regarding which there are various opinions tolerated by
the Church. The Church has determined on no
certain period as of faith, but there seem to be
no solid grounds for departing from the common
acceptation of the word "day" after the creation of the sun.

It is of faith that God created the universe in
six different periods of time ; but it is certain
that He organized matter instantly after its production from nothing.

In the beginning God created heaven—that is,
according to the teaching of the Fathers, the invisible world of angels, the first-born sons of
God, whose trial, fall, and triumphs are related
elsewhere. Suppose your guardian angel is the

least in heaven ; he is coeval with time, surpasses in wisdom the entire human race, in splendor all the millions of orbs ever made ; the sight of him would throw all the people in the world into an ecstasy. Every implement of industry would fall from the hand, all pursuits would cease, and every eye would gaze on him with more wonder than that of the man born blind when he first saw the sun.

There are nine orders of these celestial spirits, so numerous as to be simply short of the infinite. Heaven and earth and all creation is densely populated with these princes of eternity, prodigies of divine love and power.

Next were created the visible heavens — this magnificent collection of starry worlds, some so remote that, with all its unimaginable speed, a ray of light from them has not yet reached us since the morning of creation. Two glasses reveal to the eye in the starry vaults of heaven and in the rocky precipices of a grain of sand marvels of creation that fill the mind with awe and wonder.

The historian of creation and of our origin has not written the annals of these myriads of worlds that revolve in their orbits about their suns ; he gives us a date only : God created in the firmament of heaven the sun, the moon, and the stars (Genesis).

The Omnipotent created light immediately :
*And God said, Be light made, and light was
made.* This is the most sublime passage ever
written in human language. The closest ap-
proximation to it is the Apollo of Phidias in
sculpture ; there is no effort displayed in the
performance of the greatest work. At the same
time fire, air, and all the other elements streamed
forth from His powerful hand.

The divine Architect next created the waters
of the firmament, the fountains and oceans and
streams. He divided them and called the gather-
ing together of the waters seas. He filled them
with fishes of various sizes and species.

After having divided the waters God created
the dry land, which He called the earth. Here
we find three kingdoms—the mineral, the vegetable, and the animal. In the mineral kingdom
God created immediately gold, silver, marble,
iron, granite, precious stones, and all minerals.
In the vegetable order He created all trees and
plants, from the cedar of Libanus to the tiniest
herb, each in its own kind and species. In the
animal kingdom the Omnipotent created every
winged fowl according to its kind, from the eagle
that nestles amid inaccessible rocks to the hum-
ming-bird hiding its young under the garden
flower ; and all other animals, from the lion and

the elephant to the tiniest insect crawling on the brink of a leaf.

What are styled spontaneous productions, regarding which modern infidels clamor so loudly, are a mere chimera. The hair of an animal never became a living creature. Mill and the most eminent scientists of our day, in their report to the French Academy of Sciences, affirm that, "after many experiments, they have ascertained that in the entire animal kingdom there exists no such thing as spontaneous generation or production ; that all living animals, the largest and the least, are governed by the same law and can only exist when produced by other living beings."

On the sixth day, after the creation of all other beings, and when the world was furnished and adorned like a magnificent palace, the Adorable Trinity paused and took counsel within Himself. He is about to introduce into the world its king, who will have dominion and rule over all other creatures, and whom all things must serve and obey. A word was sufficient to bring forth light from darkness, and now the adorable Trinity deliberates by the cradle of humanity. He who seemed but to disport with His works in the creation of millions of systems "is collected within Himself," says

Tertullian. "*He said, Let us make man to our image and likeness.* The deliberation is solemn and the expression mysterious."

The Blessed Trinity has eminently displayed His divine unity in the creation of man. All the various kingdoms and natures are combined in Him. All orders of being meet in us. What more different than a spirit and dust? The soul of man and angels are spirits. In one hand God took the soul of man, whose best likeness is a thought, and in the other a little clay, and He united them so intimately that their combination forms but one and the self-same being—man.

It is at this very point that He reunites all in Himself, because He became man and all creation meets in the sacred humanity of Jesus Christ. *In Him, and by Him, and through Him are all things.*

The Almighty Father having created all things by His word only—the animals, the trees, the plants—He imparted to each of these primitive types the power to reproduce itself: the creative germ, to perpetuate itself to the end of time.

Increase and multiply, and fill the earth, was the powerful blessing imparted to the birds of the air, the fish of the waters, to man and all animate existence. In order to perpetuate the works of creation to the end of ages God communicated to all the creative germ, or the power of reproducing themselves. God also established universal laws, like attraction and gravitation, which the wisdom of His providence maintains firm and unalterable for the conservation of all things.

By virtue of these laws and of the creative principle plants, animals, and men, all original types and primitive creatures, are preserved unchanged to the present hour and will be preserved to the end of time. They are created by the Blessed Trinity, but indirectly or mediately by the marvellous participation of His own power. Every plant and flower of the field still, after six thousand years, reproduces itself at spring, despite of winter's ice and cold. Every animal in plain or forest, every fish that swims the ocean stream or disports in moonlit rapids, every bird that carols in the sky, all sing a hymn of universal praise to the Father of all, and utter with man the sublime truth: *In Him we live, and move, and are.*

After having created this world so fair and beautiful the Blessed Trinity did not abandon it to blind chance, haphazard, or fortune. He governs all things by His providence, presides over the laws instituted for their preservation, and conducts all to their end.

18

Providence is so essential to the divine nature, and so inseparable from God as creator, that without it He would be no God at all, but unjust, weak, and ignorant—the God of the Stoics, or the stern First Cause of the other philosophers, as indifferent to human affairs as the marble statue of Jove. To impute this cold indifference, weakness and inability to redress wrongs, or an ignorance of His own works and of human affairs, to the Father of mercies is extreme impiety.

Our Lord dwells in the highest heavens; His will is the only limit of His power, and all His eternal decrees are accomplished. *Nothing can resist Him* (Phil. i. 2). His wisdom is infinite. In a glance He beholds the past, the present, and the future. Before Him all space is but a point, all time but a moment. *All things are naked and open to His eyes* (Heb. iv. 13). *He is great in strength, and in judgment, and in justice* (Job xxxvii. 23).

It is impossible that He can be indifferent to the sins that violate His laws or to the injustice that tarnishes His works. His all-seeing eye beholds the just and the unjust, and He will render unto every man according to his works.

God and His providence are identical. Reason, revelation, and the common consent of mankind, as well as human instinct itself, leave no room to doubt this all-consoling fact. "O my God!" is the voice of every heart in moments of danger, of sorrow and suffering. This sentiment is innate, engraven on the soul by the very hand of God. It is independent of all reasoning and antecedent to reflection. It is born with us, grows with our growth, and at the hour of death is the wing that wafts the departing spirit to its origin and end, the bosom of the Blessed Trinity. The human race are in harmony on the existence of Providence, though differing in details and erring in conceptions. God and Providence are considered synonyms. Examine the customs, the manners, and the religious rites of all nations that ever existed ; everywhere you will hear the voice of prayer and supplication to the Father of mercies for protection from dangers or else in thanksgiving for favors. Not only Judaism and Christianity but even all pagan nations attest the fact. This consoling mystery supports us under all trials and adversities, because we are convinced that an all-wise God can permit nothing to happen without the highest reason ; and, indeed, He often makes use of human events to exercise His just judgments over men, though He defers their execution generally to His mysterious eternity.

His designs are all merciful, and, being entire in every act, He can do nothing without goodness any more than without power and wisdom. This doctrine was more clearly inculcated by our blessed Lord teaching us to thank and adore our heavenly Father, who directs our destiny, watches for our preservation, provides for our every want, is interested in our trials, and is the just judge of every action and thought.

II.

With the exception of some few of the philosophers, it was rather by excess that pagan antiquity erred on this mystery; everything was God except God Himself. But under their superstitions lies hidden a great truth, which St. Paul expressed in superhuman eloquence to the Athenians.

The unknown God to whose honor you have erected this altar is He who giveth *to all life and breath and all things.* We touch and feel Him every instant, because He is intimately present to each of us. *For in Him we live and move and are* (Acts xvii.) Language cannot, could not, convey a clearer proof of the watchful providence of God over every human being and over all other things, little and great. Among

creatures there is nothing small in the sight of
God. Whole and entire in every atom, "He is
not greater in the angel and less in the worm,"
says St. Augustine. Great in great things and
greatest in the least is axiomatic.

The chosen people, who were the depositary
of the divine promises and were taught by the
prophets, always adored the providence of God,
who, after having placed man on earth that he
might earn a glorious immortality by the sweat
of his brow, has not forsaken him in his trials
and sufferings.

Truly the God of ancient Israel, the God who
spake from amid thunders and lightnings, is not
to be despised: *The Lord your God, He is the
God of gods and the Lord of lords, a great God
and mighty and terrible, who accepteth no person nor taketh bribes* (Deut. x. 17). *Thou art
terrible, and who shall resist thee?* (Psalm lxxv.
8). He menaces for the purpose of intimidating
and converting the sinner ; but He is essentially
the God of love. He provides for us not only in
general and as a multitude, but singly and individually. Divine Providence is centred in each
as though each were the end of all creation.

The Blessed Trinity is not only the God of the
universe ; He is also the God of Abraham, and of
Isaac, and of Jacob (Exodus iii. 6). After having

chosen Israel He becomes his lawgiver (Psalm xxxiii. 22); He is with His people in all their necessities and fortunes; He admonishes, reprimands, rewards, and chastises them, and He interests Himself in all the trials and conflicts of His creatures. The Holy Ghost, in the Canticle of Moses, displays in the most touching language the tenderness, compassion, and many other features of this ineffable attribute. "Remember the days of old; . . . ask thy Father, and He will declare to thee" what the Lord has done for thee. "He found Jacob"—the children of Jacob, that is—"in a desert land, a place of horror and of waste wilderness. He led him about and taught him, and He kept him as the apple of His eye" (Deut. xxxii. 7–11). To teach us how to approach Him He imitates the eagle, bearing its young in its talons, hovering over them, and sustaining them in their flight.

He exerts the tender solicitude of a father and a mother for each one of us. He enables us to advance daily in wisdom and perfection, and to resemble Him more and more. After having created us to His own image and likeness, He encourages us to bear worthily the honor of our descent and to attain to the height of our glorious destiny.

No man travels alone on the journey of human

life like an orphan or an outcast. There is a Presence that is more intimate with him than he is with himself, who knows him as no other can, and in whom he confides as he can confide in no other. If there be one who has lost all human hope, every staff of strength, the most wretched of his race, even he can exclaim with the Psalmist: *My father and my mother have left me, but the Lord hath taken me up* (xxvi. 10).

Like David, persecuted by the caprice and jealousy of a merciless and powerful enemy, feigning madness and burying himself among rocks and mountains to save his life, the most desolate should exclaim: *The Lord ruleth me and I shall want nothing* (Psalm xxii. 1). *For though I should walk in the midst of the shadow of death, I will fear no evils, for Thou art with me* (Psalm xxii. 4).

If the adversity be desperate and the trial beyond measure, contemplate Agar in the wilderness. She was an outcast, refused shelter near human abode, had lost everything but her poor boy, now perishing with thirst. She withdrew and turned away her face, that she might not see his dying agony. *She said, I will not see the boy die, and sitting over against, she lifted up her voice and wept* (Genesis xxi. 16). At this moment God heard the cry of the mother and the

weeping of the child. Angels point out to this
most desolate of mothers a fountain of water;
she moistens the parched lips of her son and he
is restored. Agar and Ismael, and their descendants to this day, are mindful of Him who from
high heaven heard and had compassion. Humanity, wandering in the wilderness of this life
and consumed by thirst, will always experience the mercy of God, who unceasingly watches
over it.

Our Lord in the divine Sermon on the Mount,
in language simple and sublime, tender and profound, illustrates this secret of God which un-
ravels all the difficulties of the social order. The
lilies of the field are clothed with a beauty
which King Solomon could not rival. Our heavenly Father feeds the birds of the air; not a
sparrow can fall to the earth without His permission. Our merciful God is exhibited in the Gospel, not indifferent to His works or inaccessible
to His children, but always intimately present,
seeing and knowing and governing all things,
His care and providence extended over all his
creatures, the just and the unjust, the bird of
the forest and the lily of the field.

But his deepest solicitude is for the weak, the
friendless, and the persecuted. He claims in an
especial manner to be the protector of the widow

and the orphan. Wherever is found some desolate one who weeps unseen and is therefore friendless, God Himself wipes away that tear and becomes his friend and consolation. *I have heard thy prayer and I have seen thy tears* (4 Kings xx. 5).

Who that has not experienced many times during life the miraculous interference of Providence in his behalf? The sorrows He consoles, the injuries He redresses, the tears he wipes away, the consolation and assistance which he timely imparts, make up the history of every individual life. Our lips sigh into His ear, our tears fall upon His bosom; He sustains us when we falter, heals our wounds, turns our trials into blessings and our chastisements into mercies. How can we question the infinite compassion of God when He sent His only-begotten Son to suffer and die for us?

Grave doubts often assail even virtuous people regarding the justice of divine Providence, who often permits the good to suffer and the wicked to prosper in this world. Virtue oppressed and iniquity triumphant, the noblest efforts defeated, merit pining in obscurity or want, pampered vice trampling under its heel all that is good and great—this is the history of the world. How reconcile this inequality with a Providence so

19]

wise, so powerful, and so just? This objection
is most forcibly offered in Eccles. iv. 1: *I saw
the oppressions that are done under the sun,
and the tears of the innocent, and they had no
comforter; and they were not able to resist
their violence, being destitute of help from
any.*

A few facts solve the entire difficulty; the light
of faith enlightens all the darkness of the mystery and makes it resplendent with the evidences
of infinite Justice. The permission of evil is
based on man's free-will, without which angels
and men could have no merit. A heaven of
saints ready made is not God's plan. Moral
evils are our creation, introduced by the disobedience of our first parents, and our condition is aggravated by our personal transgressions,
for we suffer for each other's sins. A sin less is a
universal good, and one saint a special mercy to
the human race.

Viewed in all its aspects, the condition of men
is more fairly balanced than outward appearances
would indicate. The inequality is more apparent
than real—it is exaggerated. Honorable poverty
is preferable to iniquitous wealth, industry to
sloth and indolence, and health to luxurious dis-
ease; virtue and a good conscience to all earthly
goods. *Say not before the angel, There is no*

Providence, lest God be angry at thy words and destroy all the works of thy hands (Eccles. v. 5).

The prosperity of the wicked is the result of a most just and equitable law. Scarcely one ever lived who has not done some good which infinite Justice will reward here or hereafter. The wicked receive their reward in this life for whatever good they have done, and are punished hereafter for their unrepented evils.

The very best sin in many ways, and every sin is punished. The virtuous who repent, and the general tenor of whose lives is upright, are chastised with temporal sufferings and rewarded in heaven.

This life is not the end of man's existence; compared to his futurity it is almost nothing. "Impious and holy kings have sat on the same throne to show that worldly honors are not a proof of God's favor." This life is a place of trial, where suffering is the lot of the good and even the sure pledge of God's love. *Amen, amen, I say to you that you shall lament and weep, but the world shall rejoice* (John xvi. 20). The eight beatitudes have for ever settled this question.

Suffering is a law of the Incarnation. The greatest saints have always endured the greatest hardships and suffered the most. Abraham,

Abel, Isaac, Moses, Job, all the prophets of the Old Law down to the Baptist, suffered in divers ways and many unto death. The Blessed Virgin endured more than all the martyrs; the apostles, the martyrs, the confessors, the virgins, all the saints sanctified themselves by enduring all manner of evils from Satan, from the world, and from their inherent imperfections. Our Lord was crucified; He is our God and our model, and we are called upon by our profession to take up our cross daily and follow Him, because it is by many tribulations that we must enter into the kingdom of God.

How is it possible to practise patience and the other virtues unless occasions of doing so are frequently presented? It is by trial and temptation that all virtues are strengthened. The persecutions and injustices of men have adorned the Church and given most of the saints to heaven. No cross, no crown, is a maxim. *Because thou wast acceptable to God it was necessary that temptation should prove thee*, said St. Raphael to Tobias (xii. 13).

The Gospel explains this mystery in many places, especially in the parable of Dives and Lazarus. One was prosperous and happy on earth, the other poor and wretched. The rich man dies and is buried in hell. He begs for a single drop of water to quench his thirst, for he is grievously tormented in the flames. Lazarus, who, covered with ulcers, begged the fragments that fell from the rich man's table, dies also, and is borne by angels to the bosom of Abraham, where he possesses endless bliss.

There is a day appointed when God will raise the dead and render unto every man according to his works. Then will divine Providence be vindicated before men and angels, all things will be explained, and both the blessed and the lost will confirm the justice of His judgments and all His dispensations. The unveiled vision of the entire economy of their lives in the divine essence will fill the blessed with wonder for all eternity. It will be seen that a drop could not be spared from the cup of earthly sorrow without lessening the eternal recompense. Essential holiness, no injustice will be discovered in Him who will reward the cup of cold water and punish every idle word ever spoken.

The triumphs of the sinner are transitory and will be followed by everlasting confusion, and the sufferings of the just but momentary also, to be recompensed with an eternal weight of glory (2 Cor. iv. 16).

God is patient, remarks St. Augustine, because He is eternal ; He is not obliged to crowd all His judgments into a single point of time. Man must be made over before he is capable of enduring the full measure of reward or punishment. For this measure is incompatible with our present condition and would part body and soul asunder. Twice, nay, once only, has the world witnessed the exercise of God's judgment and nature itself trembled to its centre; the next display will be the end of time.

Because a nation has no soul and no future life its chastisements are necessarily limited to this. No unjust government will be perpetual. *The nation that is not holy shall perish*, is the assurance of God. The kingdoms and empires that have despised religion, persecuted the saints, and trampled on the rights of man have fallen to rise no more; decay is preying on the vitals of others and they are tottering to their ruin.

Let us adore the judgments and dispensations of divine Providence, whose decrees are all justice, wisdom, and love. The Blessed Trinity, after having created us and redeemed us, watches over us with infinite solicitude and mercy until we are gathered home to rest in the shoreless ocean of His being, man's true and only home.

The will of God is the supreme law and moral standard of perfection for all rational creatures. It is the beauty and worth of material and instinctive beings, inasmuch as it is a law impressed on their nature. Disobedience to the will of Providence is the ruin of our race. It ruined one-third of the angels of God, and such another ruin never was; not one of them ever rose or has ever since harbored a virtuous thought. All man's duties, his relations to God, to his neighbor, and to himself, his present and future hopes, are compressed into a single point—to conform to the will of divine Providence.

We must know, said St. Augustine, that whatever occurs contrary to our wishes can happen only by the will of God, by His established order and laws, and it is wise to submit to His decrees. Supreme reason can do nothing unreasonable, says St. Gregory Nazianzen. We can never enjoy true happiness until our will entirely acquiesces in the will of God, and in this conformity all man's worth absolutely consists. It consists in a disposition to do or suffer what Providence wills in our regard.

The union of the Word with human nature in the person of our Lord, the union of the divine maternity with virginity in the Blessed Virgin, are prodigies of omnipotent mercy; the union of the human with the divine will is also a marvellous conquest of grace. It is conformity that makes the soul of man a very paradise of God where the Blessed Trinity delights to dwell.

Resignation is the most perfect homage that man can offer to God; for it not only includes all other virtues, but it bestows what most peculiarly belongs to man—his will. If there be any gift strictly man's own property it is his will. It is man's essential right, and his Maker will never deprive him of it. It is optional with man to give or withhold it, and God prays for it: *My son, give me thy heart* (Prov. xxiii. 26). We should grant our Creator His petition and hear His prayer, and He will grant ours, which includes all blessings: *My will be done on earth, as it is in heaven.* Be it so, dear Lord, and the essential difference between heaven and earth will have passed away and our exile will end this side of the tomb.

By resignation and conformity we are more closely united with our Lord than by any natural ties, even than by blood-relationship. *Whosoever shall do the will of my Father that is in heaven, he is my brother and sister and mother.* To do the will of God was the essential character of Jesus Christ, His very food and sustenance; and to do in like manner is to be like Christ.

The union created between God and the soul by means of this virtue surpasses human understanding in its intimacy. Holy Writ and the Fathers relate astounding facts which imply almost that God becomes one's own property. I hesitate to repeat the amazing declarations of contemplatives before ordinary Christians. When the Jews apostatized in the desert God entreated Moses not to pray for their forgiveness; but the prophet resisted and won their pardon. God's jealousy for the least reservation in the will of His servants is often revealed. Samuel was almost inconsolable for the defection and sins of Saul. Why, said God, do you lament for Saul when I have rejected him? *Quare luges, Saul?* (1 Kings xvi. 1).

St. Bernard says that to will only what God wills is to become like God; and he beautifully illustrates this by two metals in a state of fusion, which when joined together become one. It is so high a participation of the divine nature as to invest the soul with the attributes of holiness and wisdom in an ineffable manner. Guided by the will of God, the just man is conducted by infinite wisdom and cannot maliciously err; acting according to infinite sanctity, his perfection will be in proportion to his resignation.

Conformity suits all times, conditions, and remains for ever. It makes heroic sanctity our easy and common condition, and only at the cost of an idea. It is the unbroken occupation of the angels and saints in heaven, and makes our occupation the same as theirs. *Thy will be done on earth, as it is in heaven* should be our uninterrupted prayer. It embraces all other virtues, secures perfect bliss on earth, and leaves nothing more to desire but the unveiled vision of God.

This is the secret of the peace and serenity of the saints ; they were calm and unmoved amid all the trials of life as the rock in the ocean, indifferent alike to prosperity and adversity. St. Ignatius, who was wont to look up into the face of God in the starry nights, would undertake to reconvert an alienated world if he had but a dozen men detached from self and resigned to God.

Thus the Blessed Trinity minutely presides over human affairs, and with infinite power and wisdom governs the world and all things therein. He is wonderful in all things, but most wonderful in His saints. He redeemed and saved us and made us members of the true Church, and He nourishes us with the most precious Body and Blood of our Lord, and He has prepared for each of us a glory beyond our conception.

Glory be to the Father, and to the Son, and to the Holy Ghost—the Creator, the Redeemer, and the Sovereign Lord of all things. Amen.

CONFERENCE VIII.

ON THE BLESSED EUCHARIST, THE GREATEST GIFT OF THE BLESSED TRINITY.

The Blessed Trinity and the Real Presence the deepest Mysteries—Four Proofs from Holy Writ—The Sixth Chapter of St. John ; its true Meaning—Figurative and literal Senses —The Jews understood Him literally—He confirms their Impression—Abandoned by many of the Disciples—Types and Figures—The Institution—Transubstantiation—I am the Vine, not a parallel Passage—Objections solved—Laws of Nature and the Senses—Philosophical Difficulties no Difficulties—Concessions to the Infidel—The Test of true and false Disciples—Unworthy Communicants guilty of the Body and Blood of the Lord—Taught by all the Fathers —Liturgies—Systematizes Religion—Impossible if Christ was but Man—Redemption satisfied Justice, but not Love—Merits Supreme Worship—The Blessed Eucharist is God and Man—Christ present for ever on Earth—Wonders of the Mystery—Silence—Considerations—The hidden God—Manna—The Bread of Elias, etc., etc.

I.

This is my body . . . this is my blood.—St. Matt. xxvi. 26, 28.

My Brethren :

Creation, the Incarnation, the Blessed Eucharist, and the Catholic Church are the greatest works of God in time, His most precious gifts to man, and the most profound mysteries. They are all in the safe keeping of the Church, are part of the sacred deposit of faith, and are taught by her to all nations and in all times, otherwise their knowledge had perished from the mind of man or had resembled some of the broken traditions of pagan mythology. I connect the Blessed Trinity and the Blessed Eucharist, not only because the latter is one of the highest manifestations of God's mercy and love for man, but because both are allied as the most unfathomable mysteries of faith, and are truths, not of abstract reasoning, but of pure evidence, based on the same ground of conviction—the authority of *the Church of the living God, the pillar and the ground of the truth* (1 Tim. iii. 15).

The Blessed Eucharist, the Body and Blood of Christ, the Real Presence, the Holy Communion, and Transubstantiation are terms expressive of the same doctrine. This doctrine does not mean that the priest has power to make and eat his God, as is very foolishly asserted even by nominal Christians who should know better. The Blessed Trinity is whole and entire in every particle of creation. Not so the sacred humanity of Christ, which is at the right hand of God in heaven and in the Blessed Eucharist. He is everywhere as God, but not everywhere as man. It is an article of faith, by which we firmly believe, that when the words of consecration are pronounced, by a lawfully-ordained priest, over the elements of bread and wine, a change takes place which converts the invisible substance of the bread into the Body and of the wine into the Blood of Jesus Christ, which are really, truly, and substantially present, not in their natural condition, but in their risen, spiritualized, and glorified state, in a manner suited to the nature of a sacrament. The whole substance of the bread is changed into the whole person of Jesus Christ, nothing at all remaining of the bread and wine but their outward appearances or accidents. The Blessed Eucharist contains the Body and Blood, the soul and divinity, of Christ, together with the Father and the Holy Ghost by concomitance ; because the undivided Trinity can never be separated, and all external works are the production of the three adorable Persons combined.

Holy Writ affords us a threefold proof in favor of this ineffable mystery : first, the words of institution recorded in the twenty-sixth chapter of St. Matthew, fourteenth of St. Mark, and in the twenty-second of St. Luke ; second, the declaration of St. Paul regarding its acceptance

(1 Cor. **x**. 11) ; and, thirdly, the words of promise recorded in the sixth chapter of St. John. Before entering on any of these powerful and conclusive àrguments let me premise a few general observations.

The divine simplicity is exhibited in a striking manner in the Blessed Eucharist, the greatest work and best gift of the Blessed Trinity. Revelation ; the sacrifices and worship of former dispensations; all the mysteries of man's redemption ; all graces, all merits of the life, sufferings, and death of Christ ; His body and soul in their glorified and immortal state ; His divinity ; the Father and the Holy Ghost, for they never can be separated from the Son ; the august Trinity in ineffable unity—all are compressed into a single point, into the smallest consecrated particle, placed by the priest on the tongue of the humblest Catholic at the communion-rails.

This was foretold by the prophet: God *hath made a remembrance of His wonderful works.* . . . *He hath given bread to them that fear Him* (Psalm cx. 4). Millions of created worlds do not contain the importance nor wonders of that simple act. Because of His infinite simplicity the more openly God shows Himself in this world the more hidden and the stronger is the faith necessary to see Him. Creation, the Incarnation, and the Holy Eucharist are God's great manifestations of Himself and His greatest gifts to man. The two latter contain Himself strictly.

The GREAT I AM is never more palpably exhibited to the world than at the elevation of the Host, and formerly at the elevation of the cross; the mystery of His presence only becomes more unfathomable, and it is written: *Blessed is he who will not be scandalized in me.* The Jews were scandalized at the cross, and the disciples at the Real Presence: both *walked no more with Him.*

If Jesus Christ were but a mere man the Blessed Eucharist could not be at all, or at most could be but a figure; because He is God it is therefore a reality. The end of all love is unity, identity, oneness of all existence, bodily and spiritual, and intolerance of duality. Human love in its wildest flights never has and never can attain its end. The distance between one soul and another is so vast that only the Creator can fill it. In the common acceptation of the term there is such a thing as a union of hearts, but in a strict sense it is impossible among creatures. Interpenetration requires omnipotence; it can be accomplished only by Almighty God.

In our Lord love is omnipotent, and therefore it attains its end—oneness or identity of being;

not, indeed, deification, but a wonderful participation of it, according to St. Peter: *Divinæ na-
turæ consortes.* Our Lord styles the union a
oneness with the Father and Him. St. Cyril
compares it very boldly "to the union of two
pieces of liquefied wax melted into one." We
must stop short of deification, which exists only
in the humanity of Christ. He alone of all men
could accomplish the end of love, and was necessitated to do so—*to love to the end.* The law of
love achieved the Eucharist. Where is the true
love that would not accomplish the miracle, if it
could reach its highest perfection and attain its
end? *Come, my beloved,* said the Spouse in the
sacred canticle, *eat, drink, be inebriated. This
is my Body, this is my Blood. He that eateth
my Flesh and drinketh my Blood abideth in me,
and I in him.* Redemption satisfied God's justice, but it was not enough for love, which required the Blessed Eucharist.

Already familiar with the proofs of this heavenly doctrine—proofs which are generally met in
the range of ordinary controversy—I present them
in a concise form and different arrangement in
vindicating the truth of this stupendous institution of the Holy Trinity. The promise is recorded in the sixth chapter of St. John, which
contains seventy-two verses: the first twenty-six

contain the history of the feeding of a large multitude with a few loaves of bread; from this to the fifty-first verse Christ inculcates the necessity of believing in Him; thence to the end He teaches the necessity of eating His Body and drinking His Blood sacramentally in order to be saved.

Our Blessed Lord foretold the Passion, Resurrection, Baptism, and all His mysteries and institutions; these He promised them, and also the Eucharist. Nothing was more familiar with Him than to take occasion of some miracle to remove an objection or to inculcate a doctrine that had a connection with it. Thus in the fifth chapter of St. John we read that, having restored a sick man who was in a languishing condition from having lost the use of his limbs, He inculcates the doctrine of the resurrection, disbelieved by the Sadducees. If He ever meant to teach the doctrine of the Real Presence, this was the most suitable moment for doing so. By blessing the bread He imparted to it such an efficacy as to make it sufficient to feed many thousands, not by creating a new substance, but by extending that which already existed; He removed the objection that naturally offers itself against the simultaneous existence of a body in several places at the one time. Nor can we conceive

20

anything more parallel to this divine institution, in which he multiplies his glorified Body to such an extent as to make it the food of all the faithful in every part of the world.

That our Lord's discourse in the first part of the chapter regards faith is evident from the context and His language. It is a maxim in Biblical interpretation that whenever a difficulty occurs we must find a key for its solution in other and clearer passages where it exists. Our Lord speaks of Himself as the object of faith under the figurative language of food or bread—a mode of expression familiar to the Jews: *Come eat my bread and drink the wine which I have mingled for you* (Proverbs ix.) They offer no objection; they understood Him as inculcating the necessity of believing in Him under the figure of receiving food.

The meaning attached by his hearers to the words of a speaker is their true sense and that which he intended to convey. The Jews, the true interpreters of our Lord's words, were convinced that there was a transition in our Lord's discourse, and that He no longer taught the necessity of believing in Him, but of eating His Body and drinking His Blood, in order to be saved. The phraseology is so strong, the terms so forcible, that comment seems idle. The language is so expressive of the doctrine of the Eucharist that one who believes in Holy Writ can scarcely doubt of its being taught: *And the bread that I will give is my Flesh for the life of the world.* . . . *Amen, amen, I say unto you, except you eat the Flesh of the Son of man, and drink His Blood, you shall not have life in you. He that eateth my Flesh and drinketh my Blood hath everlasting life, and I will raise him up at the last day.* . . . *He that eateth my Flesh and drinketh my Blood abideth in me, and I in him. As the living Father hath sent me, and I live by the Father, so he that eateth me, the same also shall live by me* (John vi. 52 et seq.)

It is asserted by Protestants, contrary to every true canon of Scriptural interpretation—gratuitously asserted, it must be said—that by eating the Body and drinking the Blood of Christ nothing more is meant than believing in Him, believing in His Body and Blood. Flesh and blood are not objects of faith ; no rational man can be persuaded that our Lord, palpably standing before the people in the flesh, would take such unusual pains to convince them of his corporal existence, which no man there doubted. They, indeed, believed too literally that He was no more than flesh and blood, and this was their sin.

Protestants are of opinion that our Lord's words must be taken figuratively; the Catholic Church and all the Eastern denominations maintain that the words are to be understood in their natural, literal sense—that we must partake of the Holy Eucharist in order to obtain salvation.

In order to solve this difficulty satisfactorily it becomes necessary to ascertain if the phrase "to eat and drink" had a figurative meaning. Because, if we depart from the literal, plain meaning we must adopt the figurative sense according to the usage of language. If we examine the Scriptures and all Eastern languages we will find that the figurative meaning was to persecute a man to death, to inflict a grievous injury by calumny. It was unique and settled. Thus the Psalmist says : *While the wicked draw near against me to eat up my flesh* (**xxvi.**) *Why do you persecute me . . . and glut yourselves with my flesh ?* (Job **xix.** 22). Then there was no alternative between the partaking of our Lord's Body and Blood and an odious, sinful signification which no sane man could think of adopting.

Every prudent speaker and writer will express himself in the plainest manner, so as to be easily understood, and he will avoid the use of any odious terms or harsh expressions calculated to raise unfavorable prejudices in the minds of his hearers or readers against his doctrine. If Jesus Christ did not teach transubstantiation He not only erred against this axiom of common sense, but He led the Jews astray and buried the world in idolatry ; for the Christian world generally adores the Blessed Eucharist as the ever-living God, as Christ. He insists on the necessity of *drinking His Blood.*

The drinking of the blood of even clean animals was prohibited by the first law given to Noe after the flood ; and it was repeated down even to the birth of Christianity. But, though grievous, it was light in comparison with the eating of human flesh and the drinking of human blood. *Instead of a fountain of running waters thou givest human blood to the unjust to drink* (Prov. ix.) With these impressions on the part of the Jews, it is preposterous to suppose that our divine Redeemer, whose mission it was to conciliate the Jews and convert the world, should have clothed His most amiable doctrines and merciful institutions in the most abominable language and an imagery never used but to express the most heinous violation of the divine law and signal curse of God. We must conclude that He used this language because He inculcated the doctrine which it conveys, and He was necessitated to use it because He could not have adequately stated it in any other terms.

There are rare facilities of interpretation in this instance. We have the declaration of the meaning attached by His hearers to our Lord's words and His assurance of the correctness thereof. No sooner did He say, *The bread that I will give is my flesh for the life of the world*, than they strove among themselves, saying, *How can this man give us His flesh to eat?* This objection proves that they were convinced He was inculcating an impossibility, an absurdity. This could be understood only of the literal sense. But it is conceded that the Capharnaumites understood our Lord in a gross, natural manner; Catholics are reproached for taking His words in the same sense. The question is simply this: Were the Capharnaumites right? If they were, then we are right; if they were wrong, then we are wrong also. There is one criterion by which we can decide the question, and it is very simple in its application.

Every speaker and writer has a peculiar manner of conveying his thoughts, and we can admit no interpretation at variance with his familiar custom. Whenever an objection was raised against our Lord's doctrines in consequence of His words being misunderstood, He invariably corrected the error. I give but one specimen from many : *Unless a man is born again he cannot see the kingdom of God*. To be born again meant proselytism ; but it does not occur to Nicodemus, and he objects to the doctrine as impracticable. *How can a man be born when he is old?* He is answered that it is a spiritual birth by baptism that is meant. *Amen, amen, I say to thee, unless a man be born again of water and the Holy Ghost he cannot enter into the kingdom of God* (John iii.) He does not permit Nicodemus nor any one else to depart laboring under a misconception of anything that He had said.

Whenever His hearers correctly understood Him and objected to His doctrine He always repeats the offensive expression and insists on being believed, even when the objection was only mental. Jesus said to the man sick of the palsy, *Thy sins are forgiven thee* (Matt. ix.) They *said within themselves* that He blasphemed by arrogating a divine power. He repeated the obnoxious expression and proved its truth by the performance of a miracle.

The Jews understood our Lord literally and made an objection. If they were mistaken He was bound in honor and justice to correct them— nothing easier, if He were speaking only of faith and in a figurative sense. Instead of this F

confirms their interpretation more forcibly than
He had ever done before on any other occasion.
He repeats the expressions that had given offence
five times over. The manner in which He makes
the repetition still more forcibly confirms the
literal sense. It is embodied in the form of a
precept, which has a threat of punishment an-
nexed. A command must be given in the plainest words. Eternal life is to be attained by the
observance or neglect of the precept. Again
it was delivered in a positive and a negative
manner, and salvation attached to its observance ;
a refusal, and the frightful penalty of eternal
death attached. It is in this manner that He inculcates the necessity of baptism. Both cases
are parallel, and, being precepts, must be taken
literally.

He confirms this meaning by the strongest
asseveration in Holy Writ. It is God's oath,
Amen, amen, which was never used except when
words were intended to be taken in their most
obvious signification. There is also a deter-
minating phrase which absolutely excludes the
idea of a figure : *My flesh is meat* INDEED, *and
my blood is drink* INDEED—truly, verily, actually. He comprises both expressions in the most
forcible manner possible. *He that eateth me, the
same shall also live by me.* He never would

have used so extraordinary an expression if He had any choice and if it was not the plainest manner of teaching the doctrine.

We now come to a turning-point in the life of our Lord. The disciples debated among themselves and exclaimed: *This saying is hard, and who can bear it?*—which means, it is impossible for us to associate ourselves any longer with a man who teaches so revolting a doctrine. They left Him; they *walked no more with Him.* Has He no explanation to make? If He is speaking only of faith or a bare commemoration, and in figure, will the Good Shepherd suffer them to be lost for ever for refusing to believe imaginary doctrines which He never meant to teach?

The admiring multitude had listened for three days to the words of wisdom that fell from His divine lips, and were miraculously fed with five loaves and two fishes. The blind, the lame, the sick, many whom He had miraculously cured, must have been there. They offered Him a crown, and were ready to die in order to seat their Messias on the throne of David, His father. Hearing His extraordinary doctrine, they ask for an explanation, and He only reasserts it. They dispute and debate among themselves, and are agitated with angry strife, like summer trees swayed by sudden storm. *"How can! how*

21

can?" is on every lip. They receive no modification, no softening down of the *hard saying.* They hurry away, will have no more to do with Him, and forsake Him once for all. There is an end now to the dream of an earthly kingdom; He bends His steps towards Jerusalem and the cross, forsaken by the admiring multitudes. The Catholic doctrine was just as unpopular that day as it is now, and the identical objection is made : *How can this man give us His flesh to eat? They walked no more with Him.* Whether the objection was made on the mountain or in the synagogue, the result was the same. He is standing alone now with the chosen twelve to whom it was given to know the secrets of the kingdom of God. If there is a misunderstanding He surely will explain to them ; but there is no further encouragement for them than for the wavering disciples.

Turning to them, He said: *Will you also go away?* They do not understand Him any more than the rest; they are evidently perplexed and amazed. But they resist the impulses of natural feelings and abandon themselves to His authority. He accepts the sacrifice and formally acknowledges them for *His* disciples. Peter answered for the rest: *Lord, to whom shall we go? Thou hast the words of eternal life. . . . Jesus an-*

swered them, Have not I chosen you twelve, and one of you is a devil? He saw the sincerity of their conviction, except in the solitary case of Judas Iscariot, who, according to St. John Chrysostom, apostatized in his soul at this very time and denied his Master. The "how can" poisoned his heart and ruined him. Our Lord was inculcating a mystery, like creation or the Blessed Trinity, which no explanation could bring within the scope of man's understanding. It required only the surrender of human reason to the authority of God. Had He made an explanation we could not understand it.

The objections against this interpretation are silly. Have not many perished who received this sacrament? Unfortunately, too true; because our Lord's promises are conditional, as in baptism. How can He be in so many different places at the same time and within so small a compass? As easily as He multiplied the loaves and fishes, causing them to be in thousands of places at the same time, and as He brought His body through closed doors.

Does He not tell us that His words must be taken spiritually? *The words that I have spoken to you are spirit and life. . . . If then you see the Son of man ascend up where He was before?* St. Augustine says this was an explanation for the Capharnaumites, who imagined that our Lord's flesh must be eaten in morsels, like that of animals. In the New Testament flesh and blood always mean the natural man as opposed to the spiritual, or human nature left to its own impulses and unaided by the grace of God. *Flesh and blood cannot possess the kingdom of God* (1 Cor. xv. 50).

II.

It is objected that the doctrine is contrary to reason and the testimony of our senses. No Christian has a right to consider the apparent impossibility of a doctrine, but simply whether it has been taught in the Scriptures or the Church. From the Protestant standpoint it must stand or fall by the Bible. His word is essentially true, and His doctrines can contradict no principle of reason nor a law of nature.

Who can define the perplexed question of possibility to God or understand His omnipotence? If a man concedes that our Lord changed water into wine and fed thousands abundantly with a few loaves of bread, to be consistent he must confess that the same power is adequate to change bread and wine into His Body and Blood and make the sacrament co-extensive with the human race.

We have evidence that our Lord frequently performed what seemed impossible : He walked on the waters, transmuted one body into another, multiplied bodies almost indefinitely, raised the dead to life. He impressed on the people that nothing was impossible to Him, and reproached them sharply wherever they doubted His power. Because the centurion believed His presence was not necessary to raise the dead to life—a splendid confession of His divinity—he eulogized Him in public. *Amen, I say to you, I have not found so great faith in Israel.* Now, could the apostles or can any Christian decide the meaning of God's word by assuming that its execution was impossible?

He made this doctrine the test of His true and false disciples. The former sacrificed their understanding to the divine authority, persevered, and were saved. The latter rejected the doctrine as impossible, just as at this day, and *walked no more with Him.*

If we admit only what we can understand, and assume as a principle of interpretation the difficulty or apparent contradiction of a thing to the law of nature, we destroy all Christian faith. What do we know of nature—we who cannot explain the production from its seed of a blade of grass nor understand how a thought is formed within us? Until we are acquainted with all the laws of nature in their mystic plan and all the resources of Omnipotence we must not presume to reject the truths taught by God because they are at variance with our limited notions of things.

Creation, the Blessed Trinity, and other mysteries are as incomprehensible as the Real Presence. It is an article of faith that these mysteries do not contradict, but simply are beyond the reach of, reason. We believe all because they are taught by God Himself. Whatever is urged against this adorable mystery is conceded to the infidel. The many vain and profane objections ventilated from the non-Catholic press and pulpit could be advanced against the divinity of our blessed Lord during all the indignities of His Passion. It is contrary to the testimony of the senses—this can be advanced against the divinity of our Lord and the descent of the Holy Ghost under the form of a dove and cloven tongues of fire. The senses are not the criterion of revealed truth ; their testimony is reliable within the range of nature, but no further. The infidel can make this objection against the resurrection, the miracles of our Lord, and all divine institutions.

God can reveal and institute mysteries. He has done so. And this is a modification or change of the law of nature which is the result of our experience only. It pleases God to make it dependent on a supernatural act. The effects of Baptism and all the sacraments are beyond the province of nature. Our experience in the physical world would lead us to conclude that such effects are impossible. What connection is there between the pouring of water on the head of an infant and the washing of the soul from sin? The effect is supernatural. God binds Himself by a covenant, as in the natural world, that when certain acts are performed He will give them a supernatural effect. When the Author of nature makes certain effects dependent on certain spiritual causes it is no more in opposition to the laws of nature than other supernatural exceptions.

In the Incarnation God took upon Himself our nature, and subjected Himself to its conditions in all but sin and imperfection. In the Eucharist the God-Man subsists under the appearance of bread and wine, and subjects Himself to their laws and conditions. We do not see the inward substance of anything; it is hidden under the accidents. Leibnitz and other learned men maintain that transubstantiation does not contradict the senses in any manner, as is vulgarly objected, and they assert that there is no ground for assailing the doctrine on philosophical principles.

Had our Lord said, This bread is my Body and this wine is my Blood, there would be a contradiction. In Greek there is a difference of genders between the pronoun *this* and the noun *bread*. The pronoun defines His body and blood, and not the bread and wine. An analysis of the words in which the pronoun is put establishes faith in the Real Presence.

Did not our Lord style it a commemoration? St. Paul explains this when he declares that the Eucharist is an exhibition, a showing forth, and a continuation of the death of Christ. Moreover, He lies hid under the appearances and is the object of faith.

Our Lord designates the contents of the cup as the fruit of the vine. St. Luke relates that these words were used before the consecration. But it makes no difficulty, for after the change of the substances the outward appearance is unaltered. The great body of objections against the Real Presence cannot overthrow the doctrine; they are general impieties against Christianity. This divine institution was prophesied from the beginning of the world, and was typified by sacrifice, by the daily oblations of the law. It was the fruit of the tree of life planted in the far-off paradise of God, the remedy to heal the poison introduced into our veins by the bite of the venomous serpent. It was foreshadowed by the bread and wine of Melchisedech, according to whose order, and not that of Aaron, Christ will be a priest for ever. It was typified by the loaves of proposition daily renewed and placed before the face of the Lord in the temple; by the paschal lamb and the un-leavened bread eaten annually, and annually commemorated, by which the people were saved from the angel of death. The manna that fell from heaven for forty years and fed the peo-ple in the wilderness; the particle of bread given by the angel to the faint and weary prophet, by which he was enabled to walk forty days in youthful vigor until he reached Horeb, the mountain of God, and was translated in his car of burning glory—all typified the most Holy Eu-charist, our Lord Jesus Christ, who is always with us to the end of time ; for He will not leave us orphans.

The Blessed Eucharist is Jesus Christ, God and man, whole and entire, the Second Person of the Blessed Trinity, together with the Father and the Holy Ghost.

This doctrine is contained in all liturgies, Latin, Greek, and Oriental. All the Fathers taught it, the martyrs died for it, the saints re-vered and received it. We have the universal consent of all Christian nations on this fact up to the sixteenth century, and of the majority of civilization at the present day. Up to the disastrous period of the so-called Reformation every priest and bishop ordained, every altar and church edifice, attest this wonderful truth.

A few hours before He entered on His Passion our Lord fulfilled His promise and instituted the Holy Eucharist. At the very time the Jews were plotting His death He bequeathed to mankind the greatest prodigy of His love and perpetuated His presence on earth to the end of time. Like preservation, which is the continual going-on of the creative act, this mystery is the extension of the Incarnation; it makes our Lord personally accessible to every human being. We become united to Him and sharers in all His merits.

Seated with His apostles at His last supper, He took bread into His holy and venerable hands, raised His eyes to heaven—if anything could be an effort to God it was this—He said, THIS IS MY BODY. He took wine in a cup, blessed it, and said, THIS IS MY BLOOD. He distributed the Sacrament to His apostles, and they ate and drank His Body and Blood, as He did Himself. By this act He made good His promises, established the priesthood, and instituted true Christian worship.

SS. Mark, Luke, and Paul relate the same circumstances, and in nearly the same words as St. Matthew. St. John supplements the other evangelists ; he does not relate the institution, but the promise which the other inspired penmen omitted. *Having loved His own who were in the world, He loved them unto the end;* which saints tell us means not only to the end of His human life, but to the extreme of divine power. What greater favor could infinite power and love bestow ? By the same power by which He changed water into wine, the rivers of Egypt into blood, and called all things from nothing, our blessed Lord at His last supper changed bread and wine into His Body and Blood. He conferred the same power on His priests, who exercise it daily in the Mass, which is the unbloody sacrifice of Jesus Christ, and which differs from the sacrifice of the cross in the manner only of the offering. The sacrifice of the Mass is the same act as the sacrifice of the cross ; it is the uninterrupted going-on of the same, and its application in its totality to every human soul to the end of the world. This world will last only as long as Mass is said ; when the sacrifice will have ceased the world will perish.

The words of institution are so plain, so simple, and so explicit that there is hardly room for dispute or argument, according to St. Augustine's canon of interpretation: "We must take everything in Holy Writ in its simple and natural sense, unless there is a reason adduced for departing from it."

Created language could not render the words more expressive of the Catholic doctrine. All civilization for sixteen centuries, and two hundred and forty millions all the world over at this hour, believe that the Eucharist is Jesus Christ as firmly as we believe in God and in creation. All that remains is to rest behind the power of God's words until reasons are adduced to show why we should depart from them. The *onus probandi* is on our separated friends.

The exceptions are only pretensions; they are very weak, and in a matter of natural science would not be listened to. There is nothing more common than to impart to a sign the name of the thing signified. We call a portrait by the name of the person whom it represents, and a map by the name of the country which it describes. This is very true. There is a relation between those things. They represent the objects for which they are drawn and embrace their idea; if not they would cease to be a representation.

In the name of all that is sacred, what relation is there between a particle of bread and the Body of our Lord? This the most popular objection: that in many places in Holy Writ the verb "to be" means to represent, and that it has the same meaning in the words of institution.

I am the true vine, . . . you the branches (John xv. 1). *The rock was Christ* (1 Cor. x. 4). *The seven beautiful kine . . . are seven years of plenty* (Genesis xli. 26). It is claimed that they are parallel passages and explain the words of institution. Permit me to ask if there are not several thousand passages in Scripture where the verb *to be* does not mean to represent, but has its literal meaning?

By what process of reason are you authorized to detach the words of institution from the multitude of places and join them to the few that always form the exception? Because we do not say *childs* but *children*, the plural number of names is no longer found by adding *s* to the singular! This answer defeats the objection. But to join more closely, no passages are parallel, nor can they explain each other because they contain the same words; they must contain the same idea. All those passages are equivalent and explain each other, for they contain the same idea.

I am the vine. The rock was Christ. The ten horns are ten kingdoms. The reapers are the angels. The harvest is the end of the world. These are parallel, for they contain the same symbolical teaching, a dream, a vision, or a parable. Even the sacred penmen tell us they are speaking symbolically: *The rock was Christ. . . . This is the meaning of the vision which I saw.*

God does not give us this key to the interpretation of His words. The world understands them as they were spoken. They are plain and simple and grand like God. This mystery sustains Christianity.

There are two other passages in Scripture which prove this faith most clearly. St. Paul contrasts the Jewish and pagan sacrifices with the Christian. He asserts that ours are as real and as substantially partaken of as theirs (1 Cor. **x.** 16). *The chalice of benediction which we bless, is it not the communion of the Blood of Christ? And the bread which we break, is it not the partaking of the Body of the Lord?* St. Paul describes the institution as do the evangelists, and in the same words. But he was not content with the bare narrative. He draws practical conclusions, bases upon it solemn injunctions accompanied with awful threats, using words that cannot mislead : *Let a man prove and try himself.* *He that eateth and drinketh unworthily eateth and drinketh judgment to himself, not discerning the Body of the Lord.* He declares that a man drinks damnation to himself because he does not distinguish the Body of the Lord from other food. If the body of the Lord is not present there is no room for the distinction. An unworthy participation may be a sin against Almighty God, but surely not a sin against Christ's body.

To be guilty of murder a person must destroy, not a picture or photograph, but human life. Unless our Lord's body is in the Eucharist an abuse of the Eucharist cannot be designated as an actual injury offered to His sacred person. To say that a person offends against God is a stronger asseveration of guilt than to say that he offends against the body of Christ, except by personal injury, as in the case of the Jews, who nailed Him to the cross.

Now, to sum up, our Lord promised this institution a long time before his death. The multitudes leave Him, the disciples waver, the apostles are in doubt. They ask Him what He means. He does not explain by saying that he is speaking of a memorial only, or of a figure, or of faith, but He insists on the necessity of eating His

Body and drinking His Blood. All the evangelists relate it in the same words. St. Paul, in writing to the Corinthians, describes it in the same manner. Is it not strange that our Lord and all the evangelists, writing on so many different occasions, should use the identical words and never once intimate that it was a figure?

In a word, if the Eucharist is not God, Jesus Christ has deceived the world, buried it in idolatry and vice, and left us without hope. God forbid! And why should He not give us His Body and Blood? We must adore the Holy Eucharist, as we do the Blessed Trinity, with supreme worship, and not with the relative homage that we render to the angels and saints, or even to the Mother of God.

As God, Christ fills all creation and is intimately present in all places and things. It is as God and man that He exists in this wonderful mystery and merits the homage of all angels and men. So explicitly is this doctrine taught that during almost sixteen centuries it was everywhere believed, and is believed at this day by nearly every Christian community except the Protestant sects. It is cherished by the vast Russian Empire, the Greeks, the Nestorians, the Chaldeans, the Armenians, the Abyssinians; and all these, though separated from us for more than a thousand years, believe it, as do more than two hundred millions of Catholics. Like the pyramid in the desert, it gathers under its base all the civilization and greatness, equally as all the tribes and nations, of the earth.

Jesus Christ is the living heart and soul of the Church, which explains the solemnity of our ceremonies, the splendor of our vestments, the beauty of our altars, the grandeur of our church edifices, because we build them, not for ourselves, but for God in the tabernacle. The celibacy of our clergy, the detachment of our monks and nuns, and the devotion of all our faithful are the consequences of this marvellous faith.

It equalizes all the human race: the pope and the layman, the king and the peasant, the rich and the poor, all sit at the same table. Faith, hope, and charity meet here, and all other virtues. If the greatest sinner living went to his confession, received absolution and the Holy Communion worthily, our first theologian says he could be canonized. Protestantism is a loose name. Formerly it was definite ; now it implies the thousand sects who, though divided among themselves, deny the Church of God. Every Christian community in the world holds this faith with this one exception of Protestants. So

22

expressly was it taught that it was not expressly denied until the eleventh century.

All the vast Russian Empire presses it to its heart, from Behring Strait and the Aleutian Islands and on to Moscow. The Nestorians, the Armenians, the Chaldeans, and all Oriental sects, even Theodore of Abyssinia, though separated from us more than a thousand years, hold this faith as firmly as Leo XIII. Some two hundred and fifty millions living to-day believe it, and I hope would, like me or any American Catholic priest, die for it. Our poor isolated sects have some flashes of the truth when they speak of ministers, communion, the Lord's Supper, and such other vague terms. It is difficult to believe how good God is; and this attribute is a temptation to faith, and its greatest.

It has pleased God to make this world the theatre of His most wonderful works, and He has honored some places on this poor earth with special manifestations of His presence. It is our duty to display a special devotion to these holy places.

Jacob built an altar at Bethlehem, where he was favored with a miraculous vision. Moses at the burning bush, David before the ark, and Solomon in his temple paid their most profound adoration to the majesty of Heaven, that visited and blessed these things and places.

These visits were but transitory, and cannot be compared to the real and permanent presence of the Almighty on our altars in all places and in all times, every moment day and night. The Holy Eucharist is not a figure nor a symbol, but Jesus Christ, true God and true man, who was born of the Blessed Virgin Mary, transfigured on Thabor, agonized in the garden, crucified on Mount Calvary, who rose from the dead, ascended into heaven, is adored by angels, and will come again to judge the living and the dead.

Must we not be overwhelmed with a sense of our unworthiness when we kneel before the tabernacle or approach Him in the Holy Communion? Our miseries and weakness must cause us to exclaim with St. Peter: *Depart from me, for I am a sinful man, O Lord!* But He bears our infirmities and bids us come to Him.

We should honor and love Him the more in the Blessed Sacrament because, in order to be with us, He has not only wrought His greatest wonders, but He has divested Himself of all His splendors and submitted to the greatest indignities. He is unnoticed and neglected even by His true believers, denied by others, contemned and blasphemed by millions.

In former times, when the divine Majesty deigned to visit and speak to us, He was always

clad in many of His splendors, showing Himself
to be nature's God.   Our first parents hide themselves among the trees and caves of Eden ; Jacob
is filled with awe under the starry heavens of
Mesopotamia ; Moses and all Israel in the desert
fear and tremble, and Elias is awe-struck on
Horeb.

In the humiliations of His mortal life heaven
and earth and all nature, in one universal voice,
proclaim the present Deity.   The priest holds
the Sacred Host between two fingers, exhibits
Him to us, and says : *Behold the Lamb of God.*
Life itself gives no sign of life ; He who bears
up the weight of the universe needs support or
He will fall to the ground.   The Eternal Word is
silent, man is silent, angels are silent, reason is
silent, the senses are silent.   And justly ; for all
creatures should be silent before the face of the
Lord.

But the faith of the Catholic is eloquent and
its sound fills the world.   We know who He is :
He is our Lord and master, our friend, our lover,
our Creator and Redeemer, our first beginning
and our last end, the companion of our exile,
the infinite God with all His divine perfections.
We should often visit Him, we should profound-
ly adore Him and receive Him worthily ; then
should we experience, in a measure, the happi-

ness of the disciples on Thabor; *Lord, it is good for us to be here.* The Three Divine Persons of the Blessed Trinity are present in the Holy Eucharist, the pledge and foretaste of eternal life.

In the Blessed Eucharist our Lord restores to us the humanity He had received from us in the splendors of its glory, thus fitting us to be the tabernacles of the Blessed Trinity for evermore. God bestows to us not only all that He possesses and will ever create, but His own self with all His infinite perfections.

Grace is a participation of the divine nature— and He communicates Himself to us by its principal gifts, which are faith, hope, and charity, by which, says a renowned theologian, we are not only made like to God, but He also is united with us. The communication is perfected in heaven by the gifts of glory. By these gifts we not only attain the highest possible similitude to God, but become deiform, shining like the Divinity and exhibiting the most perfect image of the Blessed Trinity. By the light of glory, continues the theologian, we are made like the Father; by the vision of the divine essence and the divine Persons we are made like the Son; by beatific love we are made like the Holy Ghost; by joy and the participation of the divine attributes we become like the Godhead in beatitude.

O happy home, bosom of the most Holy Trinity! when shall we reach thee? *Mane nobiscum, Domine, quia advesperascit.*

O the depth of the riches of the wisdom and of the knowledge of God! How incomprehensible are His judgments, and how unsearchable His ways! For of Him, and by Him, and in Him are all things: to Him be glory for ever. Amen (Romans xi. 33, 36).